Jace wasn't fami

Anchorage. "W
anyway?"

"Way upper hillside. It's on five acres, and like I told you, it has an adventure course out back." Hannah took a curve too fast, and the SUV fishtailed on the slick road before Hannah straightened it out.

"Slow down," Jace said gently. "They won't care if we're a minute late, just that we get there."

"Right." Hannah took her foot off the accelerator. But seconds later, just after they'd passed a mailbox, a loud crack sounded. A ragged hole appeared in the windshield. Simultaneously, the driver's side window exploded into a thousand tiny pebbles of glass. Scout gave a frantic bark.

"They're shooting at us!" Hannah hit the gas.

Jace twisted in his seat to look behind them. Scout had wisely scrambled from the back seat to the floor. A familiar white truck pulled out of the driveway they'd just passed and flashed its lights, signaling them to stop, but Hannah kept driving. Jace could just make out two figures in the truck.

"Looks like your friends from Fairbanks are back," Jace announced.

Beth Carpenter is thankful for good books, a good dog, a good man and a dream job creating happily-ever-afters. She and her husband now split their time between Alaska and Arizona, where she occasionally encounters a moose in the yard or a scorpion in the basement. She prefers the moose.

Books by Beth Carpenter

Love Inspired Suspense

Alaskan Wilderness Peril

Harlequin Heartwarming

A Northern Lights Novel

The Alaskan Catch
A Gift for Santa
Alaskan Hideaway
An Alaskan Proposal
Sweet Home Alaska
Alaskan Dreams
An Alaskan Family Christmas
An Alaskan Homecoming
An Alaskan Family Found

Visit the Author Profile page at LoveInspired.com.

Alaskan Wilderness Peril

BETH CARPENTER

LOVE INSPIRED SUSPENSE
INSPIRATIONAL ROMANCE

LOVE INSPIRED® SUSPENSE
INSPIRATIONAL ROMANCE

ISBN-13: 978-1-335-63849-6

Alaskan Wilderness Peril

Love Inspired
22 Adelaide St. West, 41st Floor
Toronto, Ontario M5H 4E3, Canada
www.LoveInspired.com

Printed in Lithuania

MIX
Paper | Supporting
responsible forestry
FSC® C021394

Recycling programs
for this product may
not exist in your area.

But they that wait upon the Lord shall renew their strength; they shall mount up with wings as eagles; they shall run, and not be weary; and they shall walk, and not faint.

—*Isaiah* 40:31

To Teri,

You taught me how to play jacks,
how to put on makeup and how to dance the hustle,
but most importantly, you taught me what
best friends are all about. Thank you for being my friend.

ONE

"Less than three months until summer," Hannah Yates reminded herself as she wedged her SUV between Sue Ann's pickup and the pile of snow plowed into the corner of her store's tiny employee parking lot.

Now that March had arrived, the sun was high enough to begin melting the snowbanks on south-facing slopes in Anchorage during the day. By June, the snow would be gone, the mountains would be green again, and tourists would be flocking to the store, snapping selfies beside the enormous fuchsia basket Hannah always hung out front and shopping for gifts and souvenirs. But first came the rest of the winter and breakup, the messy season when snow melted, roads and parking lots turned to ice, and cars wore coats of road grime.

Hannah managed to squeeze out her door without dinging Sue Ann's truck and opened the back gate of her SUV, revealing the precious things she'd picked up at auction earlier. She grabbed a cardboard box and carried it to the rear door of Hannah's Alaskan Treasures, downtown's most popular antique store, and Hannah's pride and joy. Propping the box on one hip, she dug out her keys and let herself in.

Sue Ann, her store manager, appeared through the curtain separating the workroom from the front of the store and hurried to hold the door for Hannah. "I hope you got the carnival glass you wanted." Sue Ann pronounced the "I" as "ahh." She had lived in Alaska for twenty-five years now, but she'd never lost her Kentucky accent.

"Thanks." Hannah set the box on her workbench. "No, I didn't get it. The bidding got too rich."

Sue Ann raised her eyebrows. "Nicole again?" She opened the box and began removing the bubble wrap on the items inside.

"Uh-huh." Hannah's sister, who had her own antique store in South Anchorage, delighted in competing with Hannah at auctions and sales. Even though their inventories didn't have that much overlap—Nicole specialized in antique jewelry, coins, and small decorative items while Hannah focused on furniture and home accessories—there always seemed to be something they both wanted. "The carnival glass wasn't a big deal," she told Sue Ann, "but there was a jewelry box I really hated losing out on. The inlay was just gorgeous. Let me show you."

Hannah grabbed her phone and pulled up the photo showing intricate patterns of light and dark wood inlaid to form the shape of a blooming trumpet vine meandering around the box. A heart-shaped padlock held the box closed. "The detail was incredible. It's hard to see in the photo, but there were veins in the leaves and stamens in the flowers."

Sue Ann zoomed in to study the pattern. "Nice. Did it come with a key?"

"No, it was sold 'as is' with the lock still on, but it felt empty. The lock looked more decorative than secure, so it shouldn't be hard to get off. There were several bidders. I dropped out at two hundred dollars, but Nicole kept going until she got it for five hundred. I told her I can't see how she can make a profit after paying that much, but—"

"She said to mind your own business," Sue Ann predicted as she finished unwrapping the top item in the box. "Which it looks like you did. I love this stained-glass lampshade."

"Gorgeous, isn't it? I got a great candelabra and a classic silver bowl, too. And a box of blown glass Christmas ornaments. I also found a chest of drawers," she added as she rolled the furniture dolly from the corner of the workroom.

"It's nothing particularly valuable, but it had a great shape and I got it for a song because it's grungy and the bottom drawer is stuck closed. Once I repair and refinish it, it will look fantastic."

"Need a hand bringing it in?" Sue Ann offered, but just then the bells on the front door jingled, signaling a new customer. "Sorry, I've got to get that. Tiff isn't in yet." She returned to the front of the store, leaving Hannah to deal with the chest by herself.

Fortunately, it wasn't a particularly big piece, and she was able to unload it and roll it into the workroom without much trouble. Once she'd closed the back door and shed her coat, she scrubbed off the dirt, thrilled to find intact Birdseye maple veneer on the curved drawers, rather than the pine she'd expected.

The back door rattled and then opened. "I know. I'm late." Tiffany, a college student who worked at the store part-time, said as she rushed in, slipping out of her coat as she did. "Class ran long today." She hung her coat and bag on a peg on the wall and ducked through the curtains before Hannah could do more than nod hello.

Once again, Hannah breathed a little prayer of thanks that she had Sue Ann to manage all the hiring and scheduling, leaving her to concentrate on inventory. She returned to the chest of

drawers. The top was solid maple. It had minor
water damage, but a deep sanding would take
care of that. She'd originally planned to paint
the piece, but it would be a shame to cover that
beautiful wood grain.

The top three drawers slid open easily to reveal yellowed vintage wallpaper liners, but the
bottom drawer wouldn't budge. She turned the
chest upside down to see if she could find the
problem. Surprisingly, she was able to slide out
the bottom divider panel without removing any
nails. It wasn't even glued. Once she had moved
that out of the way and exposed the drawer run-
ners, it became clear why the drawer wouldn't
open. Someone had put a screw through the bottom stile, directly into the center brace of the
drawer. Odd.

She pulled a Phillips screwdriver from its
holder on the pegboard and removed the screw.
After she turned the chest right side up, the bottom drawer opened easily, revealing a Styro-
foam rectangle cut to the exact dimensions of
the drawer with two one-inch holes in diameter
near the center. Hannah put her fingers in the
holes and removed the foam. Underneath, another thicker layer of foam filled the drawer,
but in the center was a circular cutout, and in
that cutout lay a wooden ball about the size of a
large grapefruit.

Someone had gone to a lot of trouble here. She picked up the ball and carried it to the workbench where the light was better. It was a wood inlay globe of the world. The continents and islands were made of light-and medium-colored wood, while the oceans looked like walnut. A giddy feeling bubbled up inside her. Almost certainly, this was the work of the same artist who had made the marquetry box Nicole won at the auction.

Hannah pulled a magnifying glass from the drawer for a closer look. Tiny triangles of dark wood edged with even darker strips gave the subtle appearance of waves in the ocean. The continents, too, were composed of minuscule shapes, with rough triangles along major mountain ranges and rounded shapes on the plains. An intricate compass rose floated in the center of the Atlantic Ocean, and a starburst marked the North Pole. Twenty-four longitudinal lines of tarnished silver flowed from pole to pole.

It was an incredible work of art. How could someone cut such tiny, precise shapes, much less inlay them in such an intricate pattern? She considered calling the auction house to report the unexpected find, but the terms of sale were "as is," which meant the globe was hers.

Hannah ducked through the curtain to show it to Sue Ann, but she was busy with a customer going through a stack of quilts. Tiffany was ringing up a set of copper molds for another customer. The front door opened and Charlie Cutlass, one of Hannah's favorite suppliers, stepped inside carrying a plastic bin. Hannah set the globe behind the counter and went to greet him.

"Hi, Charlie. I hope you've got more of those animal puzzles. We've almost sold out." Hannah reserved a section of the store for what she called "future antiques," where she sold works by local craftspeople on consignment. Charlie specialized in wood, turning bowls and candlesticks on his lathe and using his jigsaw to cut Christmas ornaments, whirligigs, and toys. His puzzles in the shapes of moose, bears, puffins, and eagles were always a favorite souvenir gift for children. She cleared some room on his display table.

"I do." He unpacked several puzzles, along with some animal-shaped ornaments with raffia hanging loops. Hannah helped him add them on the display rack. Then he unwrapped two rolling pins, made by gluing various woods together and then turning them on a lathe, forming stripes of distinct colors along the length of the pins.

"Oh, these are gorgeous!" Hannah ran her finger along the polished wood. "People will love them."

"I hope so. Is forty too much?" He pointed to the tag, which he'd already marked with the price and his initials. When they sold a consignment piece, the store kept a quarter and paid the rest to the artist.

"No, not for something as beautiful as this. If anything, you're low."

"Well, let's try it at that price and see if they sell."

"Sounds good." Hannah signed a receipt listing all the items Charlie had brought. "Oh, I got something at auction today you'd be interested in. Let me show you."

He followed her to the counter. "The Linacott auction?"

"Yes. Today was the first day. Tomorrow and Saturday will be the high-dollar furniture and art, but that's out of my price range."

"I'll bet you had quite a crowd there. Lots of rumors floating around about that lady."

"Oh? Like what?"

"People said that if a collector was looking for something specific, Candace Linacott could find it, but they'd better not ask too many questions about where she got it."

"You think she imported things illegally?" Hannah asked as they came to the counter.

Charlie shrugged. "Who knows? Maybe people were just jealous of her success. You remember, shortly after she died, someone broke into her house on the coastal trail. I don't know if they ever figured out what was stolen. That was, what, three years ago? I wonder why it took them so long to hold this auction."

"The story I heard was that she left everything to a distant relative in Australia who had never even met her, so it took a while to get it all organized. And, apparently, she had stuff in storage lockers all over town. Some of it was incredibly valuable. Just think how easy it would have been for whoever handled the estate to overlook those rental payments and for the storage facility to throw out those antiques and collectibles thinking they were just junk." Hannah shuddered.

"Yeah, or auctioned it off to an upscaler who would have painted over a Chippendale or some other treasure."

"Speaking of treasure…" Hannah took the globe from the shelf and handed it to Charlie. "What do you think of this?"

"Wow!" Charlie pulled the piece close to his eye. "The detail is incredible. It's not brand-new, but it doesn't look that old, either. Do you know who made it?"

Hannah shook her head. "Believe it or not, I found it in the drawer of a dresser I bought. No provenance. I was hoping you might know."

"I don't, but I know someone who might."

Charlie pulled out his phone and swiped through a few screens. "Here it is. Peter Morozov from up north. He specializes in wood art." Charlie passed her his phone, and Hannah entered the information into her own phone.

"Thanks, Charlie. I'll let you know what I find out."

They chatted for a few more minutes, and then Charlie took his leave. Once Hannah had emailed the expert, she took the globe with her to the workroom and began to unpack the other items. She'd unwrapped the bowl and was reaching for silver polish when her phone chimed. A text from Nicole.

Got the lock open, and already sold the box for a sixty-percent markup!

She didn't add, "Na-na-na-na-na," but Hannah could read between the lines. Hannah should never have mentioned her misgivings about the price Nicole had paid. At that point, the money was spent, so even if Hannah had been right, it wouldn't have been helpful. Hannah sighed. Here she was, thirty-one years old, and she was still letting her little sister draw her into these petty battles. Time to be gracious.

Congratulations, she texted back, before turning her attention to the photos Nicole had attached. That box really was lovely, with the flowering vine pattern weaving over the top and sides. Even the interior of the box, shown in the second photo, was inlaid with a diamond pattern of light and dark woods. Beside the box lay an index card that had presumably been inside. Hannah enlarged the photo to see if she could read the card. Nothing but a few scribbles: N, S CW 30: E CCW 45: CR

Before she could study it further, she noticed a new email. The expert wanted photos of her globe. She set it on her worktable beside a ruler for scale and took three. Almost immediately after she'd sent them, her phone rang.

"This is Peter Morozov. Am I speaking to Hannah Yates?"

"Yes, hello, Mr. Morozov. Did the photos make it all right?"

"They did, and please call me Peter. Hannah, I believe you may have a Dimitri Karas there."

"K-a-r-a-s?" Hannah confirmed as she jotted down the name.

"That's right. Prolific artist, passed away two years ago. I can't quite make out the fine detail from your photograph but look closely. Is there a letter *K* embedded in the pattern anywhere?"

"Let me see what I can find." Hannah picked up her magnifying glass and studied the globe for a few moments. "Yes! I can see four *K*s as part of the pattern in the compass rose."

"Excellent! Most of his work is chests and jewelry boxes, but every year he would put out a few balls, either globes like yours or decorative Christmas ornaments. Lovely, intricate work. Once, I even got the chance to examine one of his puzzle boxes, but they're incredibly rare."

"Puzzle boxes?"

"Yes, he made a few custom ones for select clients, little cubes about eight inches tall with the puzzle embedded in the inlay pattern. Two years ago, one sold for just under twenty thousand."

"What would you estimate a globe like mine would be worth?" Hannah asked.

"Well, if I can verify that your globe is indeed a Karas original, I'm willing to pay you, say, five thousand dollars."

Wow. And Hannah thought Nicole overpaid at five hundred for the jewelry box. Trying to keep the excitement from her voice, she asked, "And how much will you turn around and sell it for?"

He chuckled. "That depends. I happen to know two or three people who collect Karas, so I'd just have to see who wants it most. You could try selling it yourself, of course, but it's a niche market."

He was right about that. Her store customers generally weren't the sort to buy five-thousand-dollar knickknacks. She could try to sell the globe online, but that brought its own set of headaches. She would do a little research, but his price seemed reasonable. "I might be interested in a sale. Will you be in Anchorage anytime soon?"

"I'm afraid not. My first grandchild is due to make an appearance in the next week or so, and I can't miss that."

"Ah, congratulations. I can see why you wouldn't want to travel."

"Thank you. Any chance you could bring it to me? I'd be willing to add another five hundred to cover your expenses if you will bring it to Fairbanks."

Fairbanks. A sudden pang pierced Hannah's heart. She'd grown up in Fairbanks, but she hadn't been back in thirteen years, not since the summer of her best friend's funeral. She'd briefly considered attending her high school class's ten-year reunion, but with Lindsay gone, there didn't seem to be much point. Besides, she might have run into Lindsay's family and the last thing she wanted was to cause them any more pain. But she'd heard that Lindsay's parents had retired and moved to Idaho. Maybe it was time to visit Fairbanks again. "When would you want to meet?"

"The sooner the better."

She considered. "Let me check on a few things. I'll see if I can get a flight tomorrow morning."

"Tomorrow works. I'll text you my address. Let me know your plans."

"I will. Thanks." She hung up the phone. Five thousand dollars! She'd only paid fifty for the chest of drawers. A little research on her laptop verified that a Dimitri Karas jewelry box would sell to a collector for something in the neighborhood of eight thousand dollars, and a Karas Christmas ornament with a star pattern had sold at auction for a little over six thousand three months ago. Five thousand for her globe sounded more than fair. She pulled up the photo of the jewelry box Nicole had sent and zoomed in. Sure enough, she could make out a K in the design of one of the leaves on the vine.

Should she tell her sister the box she had sold for eight hundred dollars might be worth ten times that? Probably not. Besides, if Hannah planned to fly to Fairbanks tomorrow, she had more urgent things to do than torment Nicole. Still, she couldn't resist sending her a photo and text. Look what was in the drawer of that old chest!

Checking online, Hannah found a flight in the morning, but she couldn't get on a return flight the same day, so she reserved one for the next morning, Sunday. It would mean missing her usual church service, but that couldn't be helped. By the time Hannah had booked her flights and hotel, and set up a meeting with Peter Morozov, it was almost closing time.

She ducked through the curtain to the storefront, where Tiff was ringing up a customer. Sue Ann tidied up a nearby display of *ulus*, traditional Inuit crescent-shaped knives, while two or three customers casually browsed in the same area.

"Did you call the expert Charlie recommended?" Sue Ann asked Hannah.

"I did, and it's definitely the same artist that made Nicole's box. You're never going to believe what the expert said." Hannah told her all about the offer and Peter's request that she bring the globe to him.

"Five thousand dollars!" Sue Ann squealed, and the customers all looked in her direction. In a quieter voice she added, "That's incredible."

"I know. I figured I'd better head up to Fairbanks before he changes his mind. I booked an early flight for tomorrow morning and I'm meeting up with him at ten. I plan to stay overnight and fly back the next morning. You're okay running the store without me, right?"

"Absolutely. Where are you staying in Fairbanks?"

"At the Young Hotel near the airport. It's a seven thirty return flight, so I should be back in time to open Sunday afternoon. I know you have that Bible study on Sundays."

"Don't worry about it. I have Tiff and Cheryl scheduled to open that day, and my class ends at two. Ooh, I'm so excited."

"Me, too." Hannah noticed that one of the customers, a tall blond man wearing shades and a black down jacket, was hovering nearby with a gold pan, as if he was ready to check out. Tiff was busy talking to another customer in the crafts area.

Hannah stepped up to the counter and the man set the pan down and reached for his wallet. Hannah smiled. "This pan dates back to the 1899 gold rush in Nome. We acquired it from the great-granddaughter of a miner who went there in early 1900. The provenance is on the attached card."

The man just grunted and looked away while she rang up and bagged his purchase. He paid cash, took one last look around the now-empty store, and left. Hannah followed him to the door and locked it, then turned the sign to Closed.

Tiff immediately headed for the curtain leading to the back room. "Sorry, I have to go. Study session."

"Okay," Sue Ann called, but the clang of the back door closing was her only answer.

Hannah raised an eyebrow. "A study session on a Friday night?"

Sue Ann chuckled. "More likely a date."

Together, Hannah and Sue Ann went through the closing routine. Once they had finished, Hannah encased the globe in bubble wrap and tucked it into her tote next to the cash bag. "I think I'll grab some dinner at Kriner's Diner after I make the night deposit. Then I'd better head home and pack."

Sue Ann grinned. "Breakfast for dinner again, huh?"

"Kriner's has other things on the menu," Hannah protested.

"Yeah, but you're not going to order them." Sue Ann knew her so well. "Bradley is cooking tonight so it will probably be moose burgers for us. Have a great trip. I can't wait to hear all about it."

"Thanks, Sue Ann. See you in a couple of days." Hannah set the alarm at the store, and they drove off in different directions.

Hannah deposited the day's cash and headed for the diner, where she declined a menu and put in her usual order. She was tempted to take the globe from her tote to study while she waited for food, but since she'd wrapped it up, she contented herself with studying the photos she'd taken. The longer she looked, the more details she noticed, like flowing shapes along major rivers, and the way the equator was made up of several razor-thin lines of wood, rather than one piece.

The waiter brought her waffles with a side of reindeer sausage. Hannah bowed her head for a silent grace and then continued to study the photos while she ate. An alert popped up on her phone. The store security system had gone off!

Maybe it was a false alarm. She pushed the plate away and pulled up the security camera view. A dark figure in a hooded down jacket climbed through the smashed front window and ran through the store until he disappeared from the camera's view just past the front counter.

Hannah threw enough cash to cover her dinner and tip on the table and called to the waiter, "Sorry, I have an emergency."

"Do you want me to box up the rest?" he asked as Hannah pulled on her coat, but she shook her head.

"No time, but thanks." She ran to the parking lot, jumped into her SUV, and headed for the store.

By the time she arrived, the police were there. Broken glass littered the sidewalk and glinted from the seat of a chair displayed in the window. Hannah identified herself, and one of the police officers took her aside. "Looks like a smash and grab. Can you spot anything missing from your window display from here?"

Hannah looked it over. The items in the bookcase seemed undisturbed, as did the floor lamp and the throw she'd arranged over the arm of the chair. The side table was knocked over, spilling a vase and book onto the floor, but they appeared undamaged.

She showed the officer the camera footage of the burglar heading straight for the back of the store, not even stopping to check the till. Maybe he'd guessed that the cash drawer would be locked up in the safe in the back. He seemed tall, but with the low lighting, she couldn't make out his face or anything distinctive about him. "It doesn't show him coming back, so I assume he left through the back door."

"It was standing open when we got here," the police officer confirmed. "Do you have cameras in the back?"

"No." It hadn't occurred to her that she might need them.

"Okay. Well, once we're done, we'll have you do a walk-through and figure out what's missing."

"Will you be taking fingerprints?" Hannah asked.

He shook his head. "Too many people in and out of a store for fingerprints to mean much. Besides, it looked like in your video that he was wearing gloves."

A green pickup truck pulled up to the curb, and Sue Ann jumped out of the passenger seat and ran to pull Hannah into a hug. "I got the alert. Are you okay?"

"I'm fine," Hannah assured her. "You didn't have to come."

"We brought plywood," Sue Ann's husband, Bradley, said as he joined them. "Once they're done here, we can board up the window until you can get it repaired."

"Thank you. I hadn't even thought that far ahead. I guess I won't be going to Fairbanks tomorrow."

Sue Ann gasped. "Did they steal the globe?"

"No, I had it with me."

"Oh, thank goodness. Then you have to go," Sue Ann insisted. "You've got the flight all booked and that appointment with the expert. I can handle cleaning up the glass and getting the window fixed and whatever else needs doing tomorrow. Sir?" She tapped the police officer on the arm. "I'm Sue Ann Bolton, Hannah's store manager. Hannah has an important meeting in Fairbanks tomorrow. I can sign police reports or whatever you need done, right?"

"When will you be back?" he asked Hannah.

"Sunday morning," she answered.

"No problem, then. You'll just need to sign the report in the next week or so. Technically, you have a year to file a report, but your insurance will want it before they process your claim."

"I'll call the insurance agent, too," Sue Ann told her. "See, no reason to put off the trip."

Bradley nodded. "We've got you covered."

"All right then, I'll go. Thank you." Hannah wrapped her arms around both of them. "You're the best."

TWO

On the flight the next morning, Hannah wasn't so sure that Sue Ann and Bradley had done her any favors urging her to take the trip. It had been close to ten last night before the police had finished and allowed them to board up the window. Oddly, the only things that seemed to be missing from the store were the candelabra and a box of Christmas ornaments she'd gotten at the auction and left in the back room. The police surmised that the burglar had heard the sirens and fled before he'd had a chance to grab more. It was close to midnight when Hannah finished packing. Then she'd been up at four thirty to catch the seven o'clock flight.

But by the time the flight attendant asked for seats up and tray tables folded, Hannah had gotten her second wind. She nudged the small backpack with the globe inside farther under the seat in front of her and looked out the window. The braided Tanana River looped along the southern edge of Fairbanks, while its smaller tributary, the Chena, meandered through the center of town, reminding Hannah of hot summer days when she and Lindsay would float along it on inner tubes. Snow covered the soccer fields where they had played together. And over there was the neighborhood where Lindsay had lived in a rambling house with her parents, her brother Jace, and a menagerie of dogs, cats, and the occasional rabbit or guinea pig. Hannah had spent almost as much time at Lindsay's house as she had her own.

She still thought of Lindsay often. Whenever she saw kids dressed in their soccer uniforms, or came across the cross-country ski teams practicing, or when certain songs came on the car radio, Hannah would be transported back to when the two of them were almost inseparable. If only they'd been together that last night, it might have changed everything.

The plane landed, and Hannah collected her luggage and her rental car, a small SUV in a distinctive shade of orange, shivering as she did. Years of living in Anchorage's relatively mild climate had made her forget just how cold Fairbanks could be in March. She set her daypack holding the globe in the passenger seat, cranked up the heat, and checked the time. She still had forty-five minutes before her appointment, plenty of time for a quick drive through town.

Not much had changed in thirteen years. Oh, there were new buildings, new roads, but the town still seemed familiar. Out of curiosity, she drove by the house where she'd grown up. The birch sapling her dad had planted the year before they left had grown tall, its white-barked trunk thick and sturdy. The current owners had painted the house a pleasant grayish blue. Two sleds were leaning against the porch railing. It looked like a happy family home, just like it had been for Hannah and Nicole.

Nicole hadn't been in Fairbanks that last summer. Dad had taken a new job in Anchorage, and Nicole had opted to transfer to school there for the last semester of her sophomore year. Since Hannah was a senior, she and her mother had stayed in Fairbanks until Hannah graduated and Mom could sell the house, which had ended up taking longer than she'd hoped. Hannah didn't mind. She and Lindsay stayed busy making plans for fall, when they would be roommates in the dorm at Arizona State. Lindsay's mom, Judy, used to laugh and say it was only because levelheaded Hannah would be with her that she'd even considered letting Lindsay go to college so far away. But they never made it to Arizona.

Instead, it all ended that Friday evening in July. Lindsay had called, all excited. She'd heard about a party at someone's house out in the country and she wanted Hannah to go with her and some of their classmates. Hannah knew the guy whose parents were away, and she had a fairly good idea what would be going on at the party. She'd tried to talk Lindsay out of it, but Lindsay was determined to get out from under her strict parents' control. "Come on. We're eighteen. In a month, we're going to be college students. We need to cut loose, at least once, while we're still in town."

Hannah had refused to go, but at Lindsay's urging, she'd agreed to cover for her. Hannah's mom, a nurse, was working an overnight shift at the hospital that night, so Hannah was the one who answered the landline when Judy called to check on her daughter. Hannah told her that Lindsay was in the bathroom, but that they were fine and that her mom would be home soon, when the truth was her mom's nursing shift at the hospital didn't end until seven the next morning and Lindsay was, even then, on her way to the party.

Three hours later, Hannah's mom called from the hospital to say Lindsay had been brought in by ambulance and was going in for emergency surgery.

Hannah had rushed to the hospital and found Lindsay's parents already there, in the waiting room. They both looked as though they had aged

decades that night. Hannah hurried to them, "I'm
so sorry—" she started to say, but Judy held up
a hand.

"Stop." Her voice shook with suppressed
anger. "I can't deal with you right now. Not with
Lindsay in there fighting for her life. Go home,
Hannah."

Russell's expression, when he met Hannah's
eyes, held sympathy, but he nodded, reinforcing
his wife's directive. So Hannah went. It wasn't
until the next day that she learned the rest of the
story. The car Lindsay had been riding in had
gone off the road, rolled down an embankment,
and hit a tree. The driver's blood alcohol level
tested at twice the legal limit. He and the other
two passengers were severely injured, although
they eventually recovered. But Lindsay, who had
been in the passenger seat on the side of the car
that slammed into the tree, died in surgery.

Not wanting to make things worse, Hannah
stayed away from Lindsay's parents at the funeral, blending into the crowd. Lindsay's mom
seemed almost disoriented, and Hannah got the
feeling if Judy hadn't had her husband to lean
on, she would have melted into a heap of misery
and never moved again. At the end of the service, the family left the church first. Neither of
Lindsay's parents looked up as they made their
way down the aisle, but Lindsay's brother, Jace,

glanced toward Hannah. And in that moment, Hannah could read in his eyes all the pain and suffering Lindsay's death had caused. Pain and suffering that might not have happened if Hannah hadn't lied.

According to a classmate who stopped by Hannah's store a few months ago, Lindsay's parents had retired and moved south. Jace was now running the family's outdoor outfitters. Angeles Adventure Store had flourished in the past few years, and was about to open a branch in Anchorage, but Fairbanks was still their headquarters. Maybe after her appointment, Hannah should drop by the store and see if Jace was there. Or maybe not.

Hannah couldn't remember a time when she didn't have a bit of a crush on Lindsay's older brother, although she went to great lengths to make sure nobody ever knew about it. Jace, with his dark hair and laughing eyes. In her memory, he always seemed to be on his way to some great adventure, but when he passed Lindsay and Hannah, he would slow down long enough to flash a smile and talk for a moment. In high school, Hannah used to have this fantasy that one day Jace would notice that she was more than just his pesky little sister's sidekick and would fall madly in love with her. Now, she'd be thrilled if he didn't hate her.

No, it would be better to steer clear of Jace while she was here. Better to concentrate on her own business. She turned her car toward Peter Morozov's address and ten minutes later, she pulled up in front of a tall taupe-colored house with modern angles. It sat next to a forested greenbelt, and she noticed a couple with a border collie strolling down the pathway nearby. The numbers on the front porch verified that Hannah was in the right place. She climbed out of the car and was walking around to collect her pack from the other side when a man stepped out of the trees in the greenbelt and approached her.

"Hi. I'm Peter's neighbor, Jim White. Peter said you're bringing him something special today. Unfortunately, he was called away this morning, but he said he wouldn't be long and asked if I would have you wait at my house until he could return."

Hannah hesitated. Peter had her number. If he had to cancel, wouldn't he have contacted her? Then she realized her phone was still on airplane mode. She turned that off and a text popped up. So sorry. Have to run out. Family emergency. Will contact you later today to reschedule.

There was no mention of a neighbor. Something here didn't seem right. Jim White stood, waiting. Hannah eased a couple of steps backward. "Thanks, anyway, but I'll just contact Peter later."

The man moved closer. "Peter would kill me if I let you go. He's excited about whatever it is you're bringing him. I have coffee and donuts. We can chat until he arrives, and maybe you can give me a sneak peek."

"I appreciate the offer." Hannah was at the driver's-side door of her car now. "But no."

His smile slipped. He stepped forward and wrapped his hand around her arm. "We can't disappoint Peter—"

Hannah took a quick look around. The couple with the border collie was gone, but another woman with a German shepherd came into view. Hannah spoke loudly. "Let go of me!"

The woman stopped. "Are you okay?" she called, pulling her phone from her pocket. The dog bared his teeth.

Jim White dropped Hannah's arm and stepped back, holding up his hands. "Everything's fine. Just a little misunderstanding."

Hannah didn't wait to see if he apologized. She jumped into her car, locked the doors, and started the engine. When the man didn't immediately move from in front of her car, she backed up and then pulled into the street, waving her thanks to the dog walker as she passed by.

Her heart was still racing when she pulled out

of the neighborhood and onto the main road a few minutes later. Maybe Jim White was just an overzealous friend of Peter's, but better safe than sorry. She stopped at a red light and pulled out her phone to text Peter, but before she could get more than two words typed, the white truck behind her honked and she realized the light had turned green. She pulled forward.

She clicked on the radio, hoping for some calming music, but a news bulletin came on instead. She was about to change the station when she heard, "A pregnant woman was injured downtown this morning by a hit-and-run driver while crossing the street. She has been taken to Fairbanks Memorial Hospital. Her condition is unknown at this time. If anyone has information about this incident, please contact police through the anonymous tip line." It gave the number and email address for the hotline.

Could it be Peter's daughter who was hit? That would explain the family emergency. Whoever it was must be frightened and in pain. Hannah said a prayer for the woman and her unborn child. Could the hit and run have any connection to Hannah's altercation with Jim White? She glanced at her daypack, holding the Dimitri Karas globe. That was ridiculous. Nobody would go to such elaborate lengths for a wooden globe worth five thousand dollars. But she still didn't feel safe.

Where should she go now? It was too early to check into her hotel. Besides, she didn't want to be alone. She supposed she could go to a coffee shop or mall somewhere, but before she headed downtown, she passed a direction sign for Ice Alaska. Perfect. When she lived in Fairbanks, she'd gone to see the International Ice Sculpture Championships every year. There were always crowds of people there. She made a quick right turn and followed the direction signs to the park.

Sure enough, there were plenty of cars in the parking lot, and a tour bus pulled in just behind her. She put on a hat, gloves, and scarf, grabbed her daypack, and followed a group of tourists to the admission gate. A love seat with a heart-shaped back carved from a block of ice stood outside the gate. The tourists stopped to take photos of each other posing there, allowing Hannah to step to the front of the line for admission. She paid and made her way inside the park.

A wonderland of ice surrounded her. This area was an ice playground for children and a few fun-loving adults. Directly in front was a ship carved from ice. Children and parents climbed steps to various levels and then took the ice slides down. There were several photo stations, with animals, fairies, and other creatures carved from ice with an opening for visitors to insert their own faces. Child-sized saucers of ice rested here and there, and children were sitting in them, spinning on the ice. A direction sign pointed toward an ice maze.

Hannah stepped aside and texted Peter that she had gotten his message. She started to ask about his neighbor, but she hesitated. Maybe it was all a setup. Peter had seemed trustworthy on the phone, but what did she really know about him? A minute later, her phone rang.

"Hannah, it's Peter. I apologize, but I'm not going to be able to meet with you today. My daughter was hit by a car this morning, and she's going in for an emergency C-section right now."

"I'm so sorry," Hannah told him, feeling bad about her suspicions. "I understand completely. I'll keep your family in my prayers."

"Thank you. We can use all the prayers we can get. I'll give you a call in the next week or so and see about reimbursing you for your travel expenses since we weren't able to meet."

"Please don't worry about that. You just concentrate on your family."

"I will. Thanks."

Hannah tucked the phone into her pocket and whispered another prayer for Peter and his family. She wanted to catch a plane and head home right away, but the reason she'd booked a hotel in the first place was that she couldn't find a seat on a flight to Anchorage this evening. She was stuck in Fairbanks until tomorrow morning. Might as well make the best of it.

She left the playground area and headed toward the single block competition. These were sculptures carved from a block of ice around eight feet high, five feet wide, and two-and-a-half feet thick, and as she recalled, they weighed over seven thousand pounds. The extreme cold here meant the ice on the nearby pond froze thick and clear, perfect for carving.

Looking at the sculptures, Hannah found it hard to believe they were all created from identical blocks of ice. Some were solid and strong, like the grizzly rearing on his hind legs, and the medieval castle that seemed to grow from a rocky mountainside. Others were ethereal, a ballerina with her arm and leg extended gracefully, and a giant dragonfly. Many of the sculptures captured minute details like the individual scales and flowing tresses of a mermaid. A stylized teardrop was composed of smooth flowing lines, emphasizing the clarity of the ice. After it got dark, colored spotlights would make the sculptures even more beautiful. She should come back and see them again tonight.

She moved on to the multi-block sculptures, where blocks had been stacked and carved by teams into enormous works of art. She walked along the path, joining groups of visitors who oohed and aahed over the ships, castles, herds of animals, friezes, and even a life-size elephant.

Hannah thought about the year she'd visited the ice sculptures with Lindsay's family. It had been a rare sunny, twenty-five-degree day. She and Lindsay had been about fourteen, so Jace would have been sixteen, but they'd played on the ice as joyfully as any little kids. Lindsay's dad Russell had insisted on taking photos of everything in the park. Hannah was pretty sure she still had a print somewhere of her and Jace in the iconic Titanic pose on the bow of an ice ship. So many good memories.

If only she could go back in time to be with Lindsay again, whispering about the cute new guy in history class and complaining about the extra math homework Mr. Tolliver had assigned. Holding up bunny ears in group photos and making jokes about how the sculptor should have carved goose bumps on the hula dancer.

Even better, if Lindsay could be with Hannah here today. They'd had such plans. They were both going to study nursing at Arizona State, and then explore the country together as traveling nurses, taking assignments here and there as opportunity and interest dictated. After a few years they would return to Alaska, where Lindsay was confident they would both find handsome husbands, buy houses down the street from each other, and let their kids grow up together. Lindsay had always wanted a big family.

Hannah sighed and looked at her watch. She could grab a late lunch somewhere and then it would be time to check into her hotel. She got her hand stamped for re-entry, in case she decided to come back tonight, and made her way to the parking lot, just in time to see a big man in a green parka smash out the back window of her rental. His cohort reached through and grabbed her suitcase.

"Stop!" Hannah yelled. She ran toward the two vandals. The bigger guy looked up and then sprinted toward her. Belatedly, she realized no one else had left the park at the same time as she did. She turned and dashed toward the entrance, but the man was faster. He got a hand on her daypack, pulling her off-balance, and she tumbled forward onto the frozen ground, sending a pain shooting from her knee. He tried to jerk the backpack away, but the chest strap across the front refused to break, and he only succeeded in flopping Hannah around like a beached fish.

A dog barked. "Hey! Let her go!" a male voice called from somewhere nearby.

Her attacker ran away, calling, "Rocky! Let's go!"

She lifted her head in time to see him jump into a white truck. The other vandal slung her suitcase into the bed of the truck and swung into the passenger seat. The truck roared out of the parking lot.

Something wet brushed against Hannah's cheek and she let out a little scream before she realized it was a dog, licking her face. A big, furry yellow dog wearing a service vest.

"Scout, get back." A man ran up beside her and crouched. "Are you hurt? Don't try to sit up yet."

But Hannah rolled to her side and looked up at the face of her rescuer. She blinked, sure she was imagining it, but a second look confirmed it. She knew those hazel eyes, the heavy eyebrows with a funny little bend in the middle, the little clef in his chin. "Jace."

His mouth dropped open. "Hannah?"

THREE

An hour later, Jace stood out of the way, watching Hannah as she spoke with yet another police officer. She'd changed surprisingly little since he'd last seen her, the summer after she graduated from high school. Her face had more character now, the lines around her nose and mouth were a little deeper, and her long hair was honey-blonde now rather than sun-streaked like it used to be. Somehow it all combined to make her even more attractive than she'd been as a teenager. She still greeted everyone with a friendly smile, even in today's situation, while those soft eyes of hers, more gray than blue, still seemed to look past the surface and see the person inside.

Even the rip in the knee of her pants, exposing torn and blood-stained thermal underwear, looked familiar. How many times had Hannah and Lindsay scraped their knees on rocks and trees? And just like she always had, Hannah ignored the injury and carried on.

Scout, sitting at Jace's side, gave a little whine. "I know." Jace reached down to scratch behind the dog's ears. "You've been patient for a long time. It shouldn't be much longer." The police had dismissed him, but Jace wasn't going to abandon his little sister's best friend until he was sure she was safe. Thinking of Lindsay, he felt that familiar pang of loss.

Lindsay, with her sudden enthusiasms and her oversize laugh. She was always spouting ideas. "We should go ice-fishing this weekend." "Let's try making Korean dumplings at home." "Let's get a potbellied pig."

And Hannah had been right there with her, gathering the ice gear, looking for dumpling recipes, finding out what pigs ate. They hadn't been able to sell Mom on the idea of a pet pig, but they had ended up with a guinea pig named Sheba. When Lindsay died, it seemed like the laughter that had once filled their house died, too. Not that there weren't happy times and celebrations in the years since, but they all missed the unabashed joy that Lindsay had brought to their family.

Lindsay's sudden death hit them all hard, but it was hardest on his mother. She and Lindsay had always been close, but in the months before the accident Lindsay had started to chafe at her parents' rules, resulting in some epic arguments.

And then, before Mom could find a way to repair their relationship, Lindsay was gone. Mom blamed the driver. She'd blamed Hannah. Most of all she blamed herself. And she blamed God. Time and prayer had healed her relationship with God, and she'd eventually found a way to forgive the others and herself, but she still harbored some residual resentment for Hannah, less for her role in the accident than for her disappearing act afterward.

In a lot of ways, his mom had lost not one but two daughters that evening. Hannah used to spend so much time at the Angeles house, she had her own assigned coat hook in the mudroom. But after the funeral, Hannah left Fairbanks and had never spoken to anyone in his family again. It was as if she wanted to put any memory or connection with Lindsay behind her. At least that's what Mom believed. Jace wasn't sure. Hannah had always been a loyal friend, and Jace knew Lindsay's death had hurt her deeply. If she chose to stay away from the Angeles family, Jace figured she had her reasons.

Hannah was still speaking to the policeman, who nodded and finished writing something before closing the book. Hannah moved a few steps away and pulled out her phone. She still moved with the athletic grace that had earned medals when she and Lindsay were on the high school cross-country ski team. Jace approached her, reaching into his pocket to push the auto-start button for his Jeep as he did. "All done?"

"Oh." She turned. "I didn't realize you were still here."

He shrugged. "I thought you might need a ride if the police take your SUV in for evidence."

"That's kind of you." She looked toward the shattered window. "The police say they're done with it, but I've called the rental car company and they're arranging to have it towed. They offered a replacement, but I figured it wasn't worth the hassle since I'm leaving in the morning and the hotel has an airport shuttle." Scout stepped closer to her, and she smiled at him. "May I pet your dog?"

"Sure. Scout, sit."

The dog sat, and Hannah buried her gloved hands in the fur on both sides of his face and massaged his neck. He closed his eyes in pleasure. Hannah laughed. "Sweet boy. What is he, golden retriever?"

"Mostly. Also some Saint Bernard, and a little border collie, according to his DNA test."

"He's a beauty. What kind of service dog is he?"

"He's in general training right now, but the plan is to make him an avalanche rescue dog. He just had his first birthday last month. In another two months, he'll move into formal training."

"Oh, so you're a volunteer puppy raiser?"

"Exactly. I try to take him out often so that he gets used to crowds and distractions."

Hannah gave a rueful smile. "Certainly plenty of distractions today. I don't think I've formally thanked you for rescuing me. If not for you and Scout, that guy would have stolen my backpack, and he might have really hurt me." Hannah shuddered, and Jace rested a hand on her shoulder.

"I'm glad I was here. Are you sure you don't need medical attention?" He looked down at her ripped pants.

She shook her head. "It's just a scraped knee. I've lived through a few of those in my life."

"That's true." He jingled the keys in his pocket. "So, how about that ride?"

"If you're sure it's not too much trouble, I'd appreciate it."

"No trouble at all." He guided her toward his Jeep. While he got Scout settled in the back, Hannah shrugged out of her backpack and climbed into the passenger seat, setting the pack in her lap. He climbed in and turned up the heat. Hannah held her hands in front of the vent. "This feels good."

"Yeah. Twenty below gets cold after a while, no matter how many layers you're wearing."

She chuckled. "I guess I've gotten soft, living in Anchorage. It's usually ten or twenty degrees warmer there in the winter. Not so hot in the summer, either."

"I know. We're getting ready to open another store there, and I've been going back and forth a lot."

"I'd been seeing them raising the building," Hannah told him, "but I didn't realize it was your store until I saw the sign two weeks ago. Congratulations."

"Thanks. So, where to?"

"My hotel, I guess. I have a reservation at the Young." Hannah waited for Jace to pull out of the parking lot. "I heard that your parents retired, and you're the big boss of Angeles Adventure Store now."

Jace chuckled. "That's right. The buck stops here."

As far as Hannah knew, it had always been a given that someday Jace would take over the store. Now she wondered if Jace had ever resented that. "How's that working out for you?" she asked.

"I like it." Jace tossed a smile her way. "The store is doing well. We've got great employees, so that helps. Even the construction of the new store has been on time and under budget, which people tell me is a minor miracle."

"Did you ever consider a different career?" Maybe she shouldn't have asked that. The question was too personal, especially from someone he hadn't seen in thirteen years.

But Jace answered without hesitation. "Oh, sure."

"Really? What?"

The corners of his mouth twitched. "When I was twelve, I was all set to be a professional skateboarder. But after I broke my arm trying a new trick and couldn't fish the whole summer, I decided storekeeper was a safer profession."

"Oh, I remember," Hannah said. "You hated that cast."

He grinned. "Yeah, especially after you drew little hearts all over it. My friends really gave me a hard time about that."

Hannah could feel the heat rising in her cheeks. "Sorry about that."

"Nah. It was funny. And I needed something to laugh about that summer." He pointed to a big box store up ahead. "They took your suitcase. Do you need to stop and replace anything before I take you to your hotel?"

"I suppose I do, if you have time."

"It's no problem. I'm officially on vacation. Tomorrow, I'm taking the train to the cabin for a few days before I travel to Anchorage for the grand opening next Saturday."

"The cabin, huh?" Hannah smiled. She'd been to the family cabin with them many times. "How fun. Who's going with you?"

"Just me and Scout this time. I want to concentrate on his search-and-find skills." He pulled into the store's parking lot and found a spot in a corner near the back. "Can you find everything here or do you want to go to the mall?"

"This is fine. It shouldn't take me too long."

"No hurry. It's good for Scout to be in busy places like this." They got out of the car, and Hannah shrugged into her daypack and fastened the chest strap.

"I don't think they're going to let you take that inside," he cautioned.

Hannah looked torn. "I really don't want to leave it in the car, after all that's happened."

"You mean, those guys who took your suitcase?"

"Yeah." She fingered the strap. "Not to mention the incident early this morning."

Jace took a step closer. "What incident?"

"I was supposed to deliver an item to a man here in Fairbanks, but he was called away on an emergency. Someone who claimed to be his neighbor was there and tried to get me to come inside his house and wait. He may well have been just an overly friendly neighbor, but there was kind of a weird vibe coming off him, so I left."

"Good for you, trusting your instincts. Did you report him to the police?"

"Not immediately, but I told them about it after the car window was smashed."

Jace wanted to know more about this item she was delivering, but a busy parking lot wasn't the best place for that conversation. "Okay. Scout and I will stay here and guard your backpack while you shop."

"Thanks. I'll be quick." She removed the pack, set it in the seat and hurried off. Jace glanced at the pack, wondering about this mysterious item inside. Two scary incidents in one day. No wonder Hannah didn't want to leave her backpack unguarded.

While he waited, Jace checked the weather report for the cabin. It looked like a front might blow in while he was there, but they weren't forecasting more than a few inches of snow, so it shouldn't affect his plans. True to her word, Hannah was back in a remarkably short time, carrying a couple of shopping bags, which she stashed on the floor before setting the backpack on her lap again. "All set."

"Great." Jace pulled out of the parking lot. "Are you sure you'll be okay at a hotel by yourself after all that's happened?"

"I'll be fine. I've been thinking about it, and I figure they must have followed my car from the meeting place this morning and that's how they found me at Ice Alaska. Now that I'm not driving that car anymore, I don't see how they could find me at a hotel. I'll take the hotel shuttle to the airport tomorrow morning."

He made a right turn, heading toward the hotel. "If you don't mind my asking, what is this item you're carrying in your backpack that's so valuable?"

"That's what's so strange. It's not all that valuable, relatively." Hannah unzipped her pack and pulled out something covered in bubble wrap. "It's a wooden globe made by a well-known artist who died not too long ago. The dealer was going to pay me five thousand and probably sell it to a collector for around seven. But you'd have to know about the artist and his work to appreciate the value." She took off her gloves and used a fingernail to pull off the tape and remove the wrapping.

Jace stopped at a traffic light and turned to look at the globe in her lap. It was a pretty thing, inlaid in different colors of wood, but he never would have guessed it was worth thousands. "It's nice."

"It is, but you'd be lucky to get a hundred for it at a pawn shop unless the owner was particularly knowledgeable or spent time on research. I can certainly see someone smashing a window to grab the globe if they saw it, but it wasn't in the car, so they had to have known about it ahead of time. All this activity seems excessive for the money involved."

"Seven thousand is a lot of money to some people."

"True, but see that woman with the bag?" Hannah pointed to a woman crossing the street in front of them carrying a canvas purse. "That's a vintage Louis Vuitton monogram, easily worth three thousand, and it's probably got cash and credit cards inside. Wouldn't that be an easier and more obvious target than this globe?"

"I see what you mean. Are you sure the globe isn't some incredibly rare antique or something?"

"From what I saw, Dimitri Karas globes like this have consistently sold at auction for six or seven thousand. Depending on the size and complexity, his jewelry boxes go for eight to twelve, and the dealer I was supposed to meet said a puzzle box sold for just under twenty thousand a few years ago."

"A puzzle box? Interesting. Could your globe be one?"

"Not likely." Hannah turned the globe over in her hands. Jace had never noticed how pretty Hannah's hands were before, with those long, graceful fingers and nails painted the color of the inside of a seashell. "From what I read, the artist only made a few and they were all boxes. But it is an intriguing idea."

"Yeah." The light changed and Jace pulled forward. "But not worth putting you in danger. Maybe we should put it in the safe at the store."

Hannah shook her head as she rewrapped the globe and returned it to her daypack. "Good idea, but the logistics don't work. It's Saturday afternoon, and I have an early flight tomorrow morning. First thing Monday morning, though, I'll go to my bank in Anchorage and put it into a safe deposit box."

The only problem with that, of course, was that whoever was after Hannah's globe wouldn't know it was safely locked away. Jace hated the thought of someone going after Hannah over some piece of wood. Or for any other reason. It was funny, even though they hadn't seen each other in over a decade, the minute he'd recognized her in that parking lot, he'd immediately felt the same protective instincts he'd always felt for Lindsay and Hannah.

Well, maybe not quite the same. Hannah was all grown up now, and there were some new feelings mixed in there that weren't brotherly, exactly. "Just be careful, okay? It doesn't sound like these people have a lot of scruples." He turned into the parking lot of the Young Hotel and stopped in the portico by the front door.

"I will." Hannah gathered her shopping bags and the pack, then turned to look at him. "Thank you, Jace, for everything you've done for me today." She leaned across the seat and brushed a kiss against his cheek. "It meant a lot."

"Anytime." He smiled at her. Such a strange coincidence, running into her again after all these years. He would have liked to spend a little more time with her, catch up on her life. Maybe he should say something about exchanging phone numbers. But before he could say anything, she was out of the car.

"Goodbye."

He watched her through the glass doors as she made her way to the front desk and tapped on the bell there. He'd wait until he was sure they'd kept her reservation, although judging by the small number of cars in the parking lot, there should be plenty of empty rooms. Someone stepped out from between two cars at the back of the lot and walked toward the building—a large man wearing a green parka. Just like the parka Hannah's assailant wore. Jace leaped out of the car and ran inside.

"Hannah, let's go."

The clerk had just appeared through the door behind the desk. Both she and Hannah looked at him in alarm. "Why? What's going on?"

"Come on, I'll explain in the car." He grabbed

her shopping bags and put his other hand against the small of her back to urge her toward the door.

"Ma'am, is this man bothering you?" the clerk asked.

"No, everything's fine," Hannah told her, although she looked uncertain. But she did allow Jace to usher her to his Jeep.

The man had disappeared, but that didn't mean he wasn't still nearby. Jace jumped into the driver's seat and drove out of the parking lot, making a few unnecessary turns through a neighborhood until he was convinced no one was following.

"What is going on?" Hannah demanded.

Jace explained about the man in the green parka.

Hannah frowned. "Are you sure it was the same guy? It's not like green parkas are that unusual."

"Maybe not, but two-hundred-and-fifty-pound guys in green parkas are."

"How could he have found my hotel?"

"I can't be sure, but I'm not going to risk it." He turned toward home. "You're staying with me tonight."

FOUR

"Excuse me?" Hannah stared at Jace. Did he just announce that she would be staying with him without asking her? She wasn't ten years old anymore, and he wasn't her babysitter.

Jace flashed a rueful smile. "Sorry, that came out a little more dictatorial than I'd intended. What I meant to say was I would feel a lot better if you weren't alone in a hotel tonight. I bought my parents' house when they moved to Idaho, so there's plenty of room." In the back, the dog whined, and Jace grinned. "See, Scout wants you to stay."

She chuckled. "So you're blaming your bossiness on Scout?"

"Well, maybe not entirely."

"Uh-huh. Just because you're in charge of Angeles Adventure Store now doesn't mean you're the boss of me. However…" Hannah glanced over her shoulder. She didn't see a white truck behind them, but that didn't mean it wasn't out there. "I admit, I wasn't looking forward to spending the evening alone in my hotel room, imagining scary scenarios. So, if that's an invitation—"

"It is."

"Then I accept. Thank you. Let me just call the hotel." She dialed the hotel, cancelled the reservation, and assured the desk clerk once again that she was fine and hadn't been kidnapped.

Next, since she'd given them her itinerary, she texted Sue Ann and her parents in Arizona to say she'd decided to stay with a friend, rather than at the hotel. On the off chance either of them tried to reach her through the hotel, she didn't want them worrying. She decided to wait until she returned to Anchorage to tell Sue Ann about all the scary things that had been happening. Otherwise, Sue Ann would likely order Bradley to drive all night to Fairbanks to collect Hannah and act as her personal bodyguard. Hannah should probably let her sister know as well, but she hadn't told Nicole that she was going to Fairbanks, and mentioning it now would involve questions and explanations that she didn't want to get into. Besides, Mom would no doubt fill her in when she called Nicole in the next day or two.

Hannah had barely had time to return the phone to her pocket when it rang. She answered. "Hi, Sue Ann."

"Hi. It's so nice that you ran into an old friend there in Fairbanks. I'm sure you have a million things to talk about, so I won't keep you, but I wanted to let you know we got everything cleaned up and the window fixed this morning. We were able to open the store this afternoon."

"That's great news."

"Yeah, Lupine Glass really came through, in spite of everything."

"What do you mean, in spite of everything?" Hannah asked.

"Oh, we weren't the only ones hit last night. Same thing happened to Timeless Finds on Fifth, and Karen's Kollectibles in midtown."

"What?" Hannah had seen Karen from Karen's Kollectibles at the auction yesterday. "I wonder what that's all about."

"Who knows? By the way, a man came in looking for you this afternoon," Sue Ann continued. "He said his name was John Smith. Tiff told him you were in Fairbanks but would be flying home tomorrow, and he said he'd come back to the store tomorrow afternoon."

"I don't remember meeting anyone named John Smith. What did he look like?"

"Tall. Blond. As I said, he talked to Tiff, so I didn't get a good look at his face."

"Huh, doesn't ring a bell, but I suppose I'll

find out what he wants tomorrow. Thanks for handling the repairs on the window."

"All in a day's work. I'll see you tomorrow. Safe travels."

If she only knew. "Thanks. Bye, Sue Ann." Hannah hung up the phone and mused, "Is it just me, or does the name John Smith sound fake?"

Jace shrugged. "I suppose there are quite a few legitimate John Smiths in the world. Why?"

"Oh, that was my manager. She said a tall blond guy named John Smith was looking for me at the store today."

"What store?"

"That's right—you wouldn't know. I own a store in downtown Anchorage. It's mostly antique and vintage furniture and housewares, with a consignment corner for local craftspeople."

"That's great. You always did like old things. You and Mom used to love looking at antique quilts. What's the name of the store?"

"Hannah's Alaskan Treasures."

"I think I've seen it. On Third? It never occurred to me that you might be the Hannah on the sign. Are you still working as a nurse, too?"

"I never studied nursing," Hannah told him. Without Lindsay, she hadn't had the heart to follow that plan. "I got a business degree from UAA instead. I worked for a utility company for a few years, but then my grandmother left my sister and me a little money, and I used my share, along with a business loan, to start my store."

"I'll definitely check it out next time I'm in Anchorage." A furrow formed between Jace's eyebrows. "But what about this John Smith looking for you? Do you think he's connected to the guys who stole your suitcase?"

Hannah thought about it. "It doesn't seem likely, does it? I mean, they know I'm in Fairbanks, so why would they have a guy looking for me in Anchorage? But after the break-in yesterday—"

"You mean today."

"No, my store was broken into yesterday evening after we closed. Oops, I should have told the Fairbanks police about that."

"Okay, let me get this straight." Jace frowned. "Your store was broken into yesterday evening. Then this morning, someone tried to lure you into his house, and this afternoon two men broke into your car and stole your suitcase. And all because of that?" He nodded toward her pack.

"I can't think of another reason."

"I think we need to find out more about that globe." Jace turned into his neighborhood, followed a curving road for several blocks, and turned right onto the last street.

Hannah spotted the familiar yellow house—only it wasn't yellow anymore but a muted sage green with crisp white trim. Stone pedestals now anchored the base of the wood timbers that supported the gabled roof on the front porch. Snow mounded over a new row of low shrubs beside the porch, but the giant lilac bush next to the garage was still there. It all looked completely different, and yet somehow the same. Hannah leaned closer to the window. "I love the updates."

"Thanks. I needed to paint anyway, so I figured while I was at it, the porch could use a facelift." He pressed a button and the garage door opened.

"You picked out all the colors and trim?"

"Yes, and did all the painting and stonework, too. It took me all of last summer." He pulled in and shut the garage door behind them.

"I'm impressed. Can't wait to see what you did on the inside."

"Well, that's something of a work in progress."

Hannah saw what he meant when they stepped into the kitchen. She surveyed the changes while she removed her snow boots and placed them on the mat beside the door. The lower cabinets were the same golden oak they had been when she and Lindsay used to bake chocolate chip cookies here. An old-fashioned timer shaped like an apple still rested on the tile countertop, necessary because she and Lindsay tended to start talking and forget about the cookies in the oven. However, light gray cabinets with frosted glass inserts had replaced the oak cabinets on the walls, coordinating nicely with gleaming stainless-steel appliances.

Jace filled a dog bowl on a rubber mat with fresh water, and Scout immediately began to lap it up. "I'm waiting for the rest of my order to arrive," he told Hannah. "I'll be tearing out the cabinets between the kitchen and the eating area and putting in an island with a quartz countertop." He opened a drawer and removed a countertop sample showing a white background with gray veining. "Here's what I ordered."

"That will look great," Hannah replied. "Are you planning to make one side an eating bar?"

"Yes, with room enough for three stools."

"Nice."

Jace pulled out a chair from the round oak table. "Have a seat. I'll get the first aid kit and we can take care of that knee."

"It's nothing. I can clean it up later."

"I know you can, but it's easier if someone else does." He disappeared through the laundry room door and returned with the kit and a wet cleaning cloth. After kneeling in front of her, he pulled back the torn cloth of her pants and enlarged the hole in her thermal underwear to reveal her injury. "This doesn't look too bad." Gently, he began to wipe her knee. She flinched as he hit a tender spot, and he stopped. "Sorry, I know this hurts."

Scout came to sit beside her, as though to offer comfort. Hannah rested a hand on the dog's head. "I'm okay. Go ahead."

Jace finished cleaning the wound, patted the area dry, and applied ointment and a bandage. "All done." He closed the first aid kit and stood up.

"Thanks. You're good at this."

"I've had some training with search and rescue, which is how I got into puppy raising in the first place."

Hannah ruffled the dog's ears. "Is Scout your first?"

"No, I've raised two other puppies, Dakota and Ted."

"I don't know how you give them up after having them in your life for a year."

"It's not easy, but I just keep reminding myself that they're moving on to something better." Jace stopped on his way to the laundry room to open the refrigerator door. "Since I'm leaving tomorrow, I don't have a lot of choices for dinner, but I do have eggs and bacon." He looked toward her. "Are you still a fan of breakfast for dinner?"

Hannah laughed. "Yes, I am. Imagine you remembering that."

"Oh, I remember a lot." His smile slowly

faded. No doubt he was thinking of Lindsay. And about Hannah's part in her death.

At least, that's what Hannah was thinking about. Being here, in the kitchen where she and Lindsay had spent so much time together, how could she think of anything else? But if Jace wasn't going to mention Lindsay, she wouldn't either.

Jace dropped off the kit and returned to the kitchen to pick up Hannah's shopping bags. "I'll take these to your room." To Hannah's relief, he led her toward what used to be his mother's quilting room at the back of the house rather than upstairs to the room she'd so often shared with Lindsay, with its quirky dormer window over-looking the street out front.

The old sewing room now contained a Crafts-man-style daybed, covered with a log cabin quilt in shades of blue, green, and coral. A small table with a sewing machine remained on the far wall, but the quilting frame and large cabinet that used to hold fabrics of every imaginable color were gone. "Mom and Dad usually come up for a month or so in the summer," Jace explained, "and Mom can't go without sewing for that long, so she keeps a machine here."

"It's nice that they have a place to come back to." Hannah set her pack on the chair next to the sewing table and ran her finger over the tiny hand stitches in the quilt on the bed. "Your mom is so talented."

"I know. Her latest project is making lap quilts for people in nursing homes." He placed the shopping bags next to the pack. "Okay, well, I need to get a couple more things packed for the cabin. You know where the bathrooms are and everything. Let's plan to eat in about an hour. Okay?"

"Sounds good. Thank you again, Jace."

He waved away her thanks and she was left alone with her thoughts for the first time since surprising the thieves in the parking lot. She changed from her torn pants to the bulky gray sweatpants she'd picked up at the store. They looked ridiculous with her dressy black sweater, but they would do until she could get home. It only took a minute to arrange the basic toiletries she'd purchased on the counter of the bathroom across the hall. She returned to her room, unwrapped the globe, and sat down on the daybed while she examined it.

Could Jace be right that it was a puzzle box? The ones Peter had mentioned were cubes, but he'd also said they were custom-made for select clients, so it was certainly possible that someone, possibly Candace Linacott herself, had commissioned a puzzle globe. If this was a one-of-a-kind Karas puzzle box, it might well be worth far more than either she or Peter had realized, assuming anyone knew of its existence. But as she turned the globe over in her hands, she couldn't see any visible openings or other clues that would lead her to believe it wasn't a solid piece.

After a soft knock on the open door, Jace appeared, holding a yellow sticky note. "Hi. It just occurred to me that you might want the Wi-Fi passcode for your phone."

"Thanks." She reached out and accepted the note.

He noticed her torn pants, folded on the bed. "Want me to throw those in the wash for you?"

"No, they have to be dry-cleaned, and besides, they're ruined. Throw them away, unless you think your mom might use the wool flannel in a quilt."

"I'm sure she could. You know how she hates to throw away good fabric." He nodded at the globe in her hands. "May I see it?"

"Of course." She handed him the globe. "See the letter K worked into the design on the compass rose? That's a signature for this artist."

"Neat." He sat at the desk chair and ran a finger over the smooth surface of the Pacific Ocean. "Where did you get it, anyway?"

"At an auction. Candace Linacott, who was a well-known antiques dealer and collector in Anchorage, passed away three years ago, but they just held the estate auction on Friday."

"Candace Linacott." Jace tapped his finger against his chin. "That name sounds familiar. Wasn't she involved in some scandal years ago? Something to do with gold coins stolen at the Anchorage airport. Or was it walrus ivory?"

"Walrus ivory," Hannah confirmed. "I'd forgotten about that. Her employee was caught at the airport trying to pick up a bunch of illegal carvings. Only Alaska natives are allowed to carve walrus ivory, but there was some scheme to export the ivory, have the carving done overseas, and then claim it was genuine Alaskan native art. The police didn't charge her, though. As I recall, she convinced the investigators that she was a victim of the scheme, rather than a collaborator. The gold coins were a year or two before that."

"That's right. That was the one where they found a courier in one of the bathroom stalls, drugged and unconscious, and the gold coins he'd been carrying were gone."

Hannah nodded. "My eighth-grade history teacher was fascinated with that whole story and kept us up to date with all the details. There were five coins in the collection, I believe, all very rare. The courier was just changing planes in Anchorage, on his way to deliver them to a museum on the East Coast. He said he couldn't remember anything about the assault. The kids in my history class were divided on whether he was in on the heist or not, but my teacher pointed out that he was drugged, so it wasn't surprising his memory was foggy. Later, an airline employee who police identified as a 'person of interest' was found dead. But Ms. Linacott didn't have any connection with that one, as far as I know."

Jace raised his eyebrows. "I didn't realize the antiques and collectibles business was so dangerous."

Hannah laughed. "Ordinarily, the biggest danger I face is throwing out my back trying to move some heavy piece of furniture, but I suppose anytime someone has something valuable, there are people who want to take it away."

Jace turned the globe over to look at the Antarctic end. "So you bought this on Friday at the auction, and your store was broken into that night?"

"Yes. Actually, I didn't exactly buy the globe. I bought a chest of drawers, and it was inside."

"Like someone had forgotten it was there?"

"No, much more deliberate. The drawer had a foam insert and it had been screwed shut. Whoever put it there was hiding the globe."

Jace frowned. "Do you think it was Candace Linacott?"

"Who else would it be? The chest itself wasn't particularly valuable, at least compared to most of the antique furniture in her house. In fact, considering how grimy and neglected it looked, I'm sure it wasn't in her house. It must have been found in a storage unit. She had units rented all over town."

"Why would she rent storage units all over town?" Jace asked.

"Presumably because she didn't have room for all her stuff."

"But why all over?" Jace continued. "Why not rent multiple units at the same place?"

Hannah sat up straighter. "To make it harder for someone to find something she'd hidden there?"

"That was my first thought." He handed her the globe. "Better wrap this up again and keep it safe until we can figure out why these guys want it so badly."

FIVE

The next morning, Hannah woke up early. She showered and used the blow-dryer she found in the bathroom drawer to dry her hair. Since her straightening iron and makeup had been in the stolen suitcase, her morning routine was reduced to tying her hair back in a ponytail and getting dressed. At least she had clean underwear, thanks to the three-pack she'd picked up at the box store yesterday. She tucked the comb and toiletries she'd bought into her daypack along with the globe.

The scent of coffee lured her to the kitchen, where she found Jace pouring batter onto a griddle. "Pancakes!" Hannah exclaimed. "I haven't had those in ages."

"Blueberry pancakes." Jace sprinkled frozen wild berries evenly over the cooking pancakes. "There's coffee in the pot. Could you get the orange juice from the fridge and syrup from the pantry, please?"

"Sure." Hannah retrieved those items and set forks, napkins, and juice glasses on the table before filling a mug and taking her first sip of coffee.

Jace flipped the pancakes. "You said your flight is at seven thirty, right? I'll plan to drop you at the airport on my way to the train station, if that works for you."

"That's perfect. Thanks."

"It's no problem. Could you hand me some plates?"

Hannah retrieved two plates from the cabinet where they'd always been, and Jace served up the pancakes. He poured himself a second cup of coffee, stirring in a spoonful of sugar before sitting down at the table. He bowed his head. "Lord, we thank You for Your blessings and for this food. Keep us safe as we travel, and especially watch over Hannah. In Your name. Amen." He smiled at Hannah and picked up his fork.

Hannah tried to remember the last time she'd shared a home-cooked breakfast with someone. Even when she visited her parents in Arizona, they usually just helped themselves to coffee and pastries at their own convenience rather than sit down together. There was something very intimate about sharing the first meal of the day. But at the same time, she couldn't help noticing all the empty chairs around the oak table and thinking of the people who used to fill them.

Once they'd finished breakfast, Hannah offered to wash up while Jace transferred the last few items from the refrigerator into his ice chest and then loaded it into his Jeep. Scout, already in his service vest, followed on his heels, obviously worried that he might be inadvertently left behind. Hannah was just wiping the last plate and returning it to the cupboard when Jace stepped inside. "Looks like we're all set. Are you ready to go?"

It felt wrong, leaving Lindsay's house without even mentioning her name, but Hannah was taking her lead from Jace. If he didn't want to talk about Lindsay, she wouldn't push it. So she just smiled and hoisted her daypack over one shoulder. "Ready." But as she walked to the garage, she said a silent prayer of thanks for the wonderful memories made in this house, for sending Jace to her yesterday just when she'd needed him, and for the blessing of growing up with Lindsay as a best friend.

This early on a Sunday morning, there was little traffic on the road. They made their way through town and were almost to the airport, driving along next to a relatively deserted portion of the road when their headlights picked up something ahead. "What is that?"

As they drew closer, it became obvious. A car was parked across the road, blocking both lanes. Jace slowed the Jeep to a crawl. "That's strange. Do you see anybody? You'd think if they broke down, they'd leave their flashers—" Scout suddenly began barking. Jace glanced into his rearview mirror and jerked the steering wheel to the right. "Hang on!" He pulled the Jeep across the ditch and into the field. Scout let out a startled yelp.

"What are you doing?" Hannah yelled.

"That white truck is behind us."

Hannah looked back to see the truck racing up the road toward them. Jace maneuvered around the abandoned car and back onto the road on the other side. The white truck did the same, but it had to slow down to make its way across the ditches, which gave Jace time to speed away, turn off the main road, and wind through a couple of neighborhoods. He finally pulled into the parking lot of an empty store and parked behind a Dumpster. When he turned to look at Hannah, he was breathing hard. "Did you get a license plate number?"

"No." She hadn't even thought of it. She put her hand over her still-racing heart.

"I didn't either. These people are serious, Hannah. You'd better call the police. Or maybe we should just go to the station."

"No. You saw yesterday—these things take hours. I'd miss my flight. Worse, you'd miss your train, and it only runs once a week."

"Yeah, but—"

"It's fine. I'll call from Anchorage and report it. It's not like we have the plate number or anything that could really help them, and they already know about the white pickup truck. Just drop me at the airport."

"I'm not going to do that." His face was set in stone.

"What? Why?"

"It's not safe. Think about it, Hannah. They knew you would be coming to the airport, and when. They couldn't have left that car in the middle of the road for very long, or the police would have been there. They must have been watching for you to drive by and called ahead to have someone set the trap."

"But airports are public places with lots of security. I'll be safe there."

"What about when you get home to Anchorage? Are you parked at the airport there? What if they jump you on the way to your car? Or follow you home?"

"Mine is the first flight of the day. They can't beat me back to Anchorage."

"They can't, but what if they're working with John Smith, or someone else you don't know about?" Jace paused briefly. "You need to ride the train with me."

"The train? How would that help?"

"It's going to Anchorage, too. You'd still get there today, but they wouldn't know you were coming."

"But I'm scheduled to work at the store this afternoon," Hannah protested.

"Surely you have some system for when people call in sick or have an emergency and can't show up."

"Of course we do. I just—" She studied his determined face for a moment. "You're not going to budge on this, are you?"

He shook his head. "Nope."

"Okay, fine. I'll ride the train with you and Scout." At least that way, he would still get his vacation at the cabin, and she would still get home.

"Good." He glanced at his watch. "We have just enough time for a quick stop before we go to the train station."

A few minutes later, they were circling behind Jace's family's store. He pulled into a narrow drive labeled Private and swiped a card through a box there. The barrier rose, and he continued down the ramp to the basement parking garage. It was one of the many perks enjoyed by employees of the Angeles Adventure Store, as Hannah knew since she'd worked there part-time for two summers. "Come on in," he told her. "I just need to pick up a few things for my trip to the cabin."

"Okay." Hannah grabbed the daypack, not daring to leave it alone even in a secure parking garage, and followed Jace and Scout to the elevator. Jace's was the only car there, but of course it was too early to be open, and besides, it was Sunday. "Are you still closed on Sundays?" she asked as the elevator doors closed.

"Yes. Mom and Dad started the tradition, I've decided to keep it that way. The employees appreciate having the day off." The doors opened and they stepped into the employee break room. Jace led them through a swinging door into the main store. Fishing gear filled the section to their right, tents and camping equipment to the left. Jace headed toward a desk at the back marked Rentals, next to the outdoor clothing section. Another employee perk, Hannah remembered—free rental of the latest outdoor equipment. "Why don't you wait here?" Jace suggested. "I just need to sign out a couple of things for the trip."

"Okay. While you do that, I can cancel my flight." She took care of that and also texted Sue Ann that she was taking the train and wouldn't be in this afternoon after all since she wouldn't arrive until after closing time. Ordinarily she would call, but it was early, and Sue Ann might still be sleeping. Jace and Scout weren't back yet, so she wandered around the store. The old speckled beige tiles on the floor had been replaced with faux wood vinyl planks, and the signage had been updated, but all the departments were still in the same places, and a photo of the store from about fifty years ago still hung on the wall behind the customer service desk, alongside the framed first dollar Jace's parents had earned there.

Jace returned carrying a bulging backpack and a ski bag. Hannah was surprised, since she'd already seen him putting another ski bag into the storage box mounted on the top rack of his Jeep, but she figured maybe he wanted different skis. "Are you ready?"

"All set." They returned to the garage and drove to the train station without incident. Hannah noticed that Jace rejected a couple of parking spaces toward the front of the lot and instead parked between a van and a big truck in the back. Good thinking. Whoever had blocked the road this morning had presumably noted what kind of car they were driving. No use making it easy to find. Jace took a plastic sled from the back of the car and stacked it with an ice chest, a duffel, and the backpack he'd picked up at the store. That left Hannah to carry the ski bags while he dragged the heavy sled along the snow at the edge of the parking lot. A brisk breeze cut through Hannah's sweatpants, and she hurried forward, eager to reach the warm station.

It took a while to buy Hannah a ticket and get Jace's luggage checked in, but before too long, they were boarding the train. Scout, as a service dog in training, was allowed to ride with them in their car, rather than in a crate in the baggage car where pets were normally transported. The dog stretched out in the area in front of their seats and prepared to nap.

Soon they were swaying gently along the tracks. Pristine snow blanketed the ground outside. They passed frozen creeks, twisting and winding through groves of white-barked birch trees and clusters of spruce, their branches drooping gracefully under heavy loads of snow. As they drew closer to Denali National Park, flashes of the snow-covered mountains appeared whenever they passed gaps in the trees.

They broke out into an open area, and there was Denali, the highest mountain in North America. Clouds clung to the sides like fluffy bits of cotton caught on the jagged rocks, but the snow-covered peak rose above them, almost appearing to float in the sky. "Wow," Hannah whispered, never taking her eyes off the mountain until the train curved into the woods and it disappeared. "What a view."

Jace grinned. "Aren't you glad you decided to take the train with me instead of flying?"

"I am," she admitted. When they hit another clear area, more clouds had gathered, obscuring the mountain, but Hannah would never forget that magical glimpse of Denali. God's creation was every bit as inspiring as a church service. In fact, Hannah was having such a wonderful time, she'd almost forgotten why she was on the train in the first place.

A train employee came through to tell them the dining car was open for lunch. They found a table with a view on the west side of the train, and Scout settled under the table. Hannah set her pack beside her on the seat. After looking over the menu, they both ordered seafood chowder, which arrived promptly. They had just finished saying grace and started to eat when Hannah's phone chimed twice, and then twice more.

'I'm surprised we have a signal," Jace commented, as he passed the breadbasket to Hannah.

"Just one bar." Hannah took a slice of sourdough bread and set it on the plate beside her bowl of salmon chowder. "Sue Ann said that blond man was back. Tiff told him my train wasn't coming in until late and he said he'd be back tomorrow." She flicked to the next message. "That's odd. The other three are from my sister, asking me to call her."

"Why is that odd? Don't you usually call your sister?"

"Not really. We're on more of an occasional text basis." Which was sad when Hannah thought about it. She and Nicole had somehow reached the point where their relationship was nothing but competition over the occasional antique. That just wasn't right. "Three texts, about fifteen minutes apart. I hope nothing bad has happened." She dialed, but even as she pressed the button, the one bar on her phone disappeared. "No good. I've lost my signal."

"We should pick it up again around Cantwell in about an hour. What is Nicole up to these days, anyway?" It was an obvious ploy to get her mind off possible disaster scenarios, but Hannah took the bait.

"Nicole has an antique shop, too."

"Really? I remember you were always fascinated by history and old things, but I never realized your sister was, as well."

Hannah gave a rueful smile. "I don't think she was, back then. It wasn't until I opened my store that she suddenly developed an interest."

"Hmm, sort of like the way she decided to try out for the biathlon team after you and Lindsay did? As I recall, that didn't go well for her."

"No, it didn't." As a freshman, Nicole was a decent cross-country skier, but she hadn't been putting in the hours Lindsay and Hannah had, as members of the varsity team. She had been so winded during biathlon tryouts, trying to keep up with the group, that she'd been unable to hold her rifle steady and had missed every single target. Somehow, in Nicole's mind, her humiliation had been Hannah's fault. "Now that you mention it, maybe that's why she was so eager to open a store like mine, only better."

"Better?"

"Different, anyway. More upscale. Her store is in South Anchorage, in a custom-designed building that looks like a Swiss chalet. She specializes in jewelry, coins, and decorative items, rather than housewares like mine."

"How did she afford a custom-designed store?"

"She was married to a very successful contractor at the time, and he built it for her and set her up in business."

"*Was* married?"

"She's divorced now. Turns out part of the reason her husband encouraged her to start her own store was to keep her occupied so she wouldn't notice how much time he was spending elsewhere. But about a year after she opened the store, his office manager turned up pregnant and he asked Nicole for a divorce."

"What a louse."

"No argument here. But to give Nicole credit, she's landed on her feet. She still lives in the house he built for them on the hillside, complete with a movie theater, ten-person hot tub, and an adventure course on the premises he built for his two teenagers from a prior marriage. Nicole stayed on good terms with them and let them continue to use the course even after the divorce, but they've both moved out of state now. She put in lots of effort to learn all about antiques, and her store seems to be thriving." Hannah smiled. "But then, so is mine."

"So who is winning the antiques competition?"

"I guess that depends on the day. As I said, we mostly carry different inventories, but there's sometimes overlap. At the Linacott auction, for example, I bid on some carnival glass, but Nicole bid it up to the point where I had to drop out, even though that's not something she would usually carry. Sisters!" she exclaimed in exasperation, but then it hit her. Here she was, complaining about Nicole when Jace had lost his only sister, and it was at least partially Hannah's fault.

She glanced at Jace, looking for signs of hurt, but he didn't seem to be thinking about Lindsay right then. "Did you buy anything besides the chest of drawers that had the globe inside?" he asked.

"A few nice things. A stained-glass lampshade, Christmas ornaments, a candelabra, a silver bowl. Oh, and there was another marquetry jewelry box that I now realize was a Dimitri Karas like the globe. Nicole outbid me on that one as well. Let me show you." She found the texts with the photos and handed the phone to him.

"Beautiful. Hey, she says she sold the box the same day she bought it. Isn't that unusual?"

Hannah shrugged. "It happens to me occasionally." But then she realized what Jace was getting at. "Do you think her quick sale might be related to these attempts to snatch the globe?"

"I wonder. Would she have a record of who she sold it to?"

"I don't know. It's possible."

"Why don't you ask her about it when you return her call?" Jace suggested.

"I'll do that. At the very least, maybe she can describe the customer."

They finished their lunch and returned to their seats. Before long, an announcement came over the loudspeaker, "We're crossing Ciamruq Bridge, the second-highest crossing on our trip today. If you look out to the right, you'll get a beautiful view of the Ciamruq River."

Jace leaned forward to peer out the window.

"Oh, look. Three, no, four moose are walking along beside the river way down there."

Hannah gave a quick glance, but as always, the distance to the ground made her stomach clench. She closed her eyes and drew in a deep breath, silently counting to four, then exhaling to the count of four. Three breaths later, Jace touched her arm. "It's okay. We're past the bridge."

She smiled at him. "Thanks."

"Still not a fan of heights, huh?"

"Nope." She'd missed out on quite a few popular hikes because she couldn't make herself walk along ledges, no matter how broad they were. "I've tried. I know in my mind I'm perfectly safe, but the rest of me is convinced I'll fall to my death."

"I get it. There's nothing rational about phobias. For me, it's snakes. I was going to share an apartment with this guy in college until I found out he had a pet boa constrictor." He shuddered. "No way was I going to room with a legless reptile."

Hannah had a feeling Jace was exaggerating to make her feel better, but she appreciated it. "Good thing you live in Alaska, then, where we don't have any reptiles."

"Absolutely. I'll take earthquakes, volcanoes, and grizzlies over rattlesnakes any day."

Hannah checked her phone again, but there

was still no signal. She kept checking every fifteen minutes or so, until she finally spotted two bars. She was about to dial Nicole's number when her phone rang. Her sister had beat her to it.

"Hannah, I've been trying to reach you all day." The hollow sound of her voice indicated that Nicole was on speaker phone.

"I'm sorry. I've been out of cell phone range. What's wrong?"

"Nothing's wrong," Nicole declared, but her voice said otherwise. "I just need you to come to my house."

"Why? Is it about Mom or Dad?" She and Nicole seldom came to each other's homes except when their parents came to visit. Sad but true.

"No, it's not about them," Nicole answered. "I just need you to come here, right away.

"I can't. I'm on a train."

"What in the world are you doing on a train?" Nicole almost shrieked, as though Hannah had chosen the train for the sole purpose of ruining her plans.

Hannah doubted whatever Nicole was upset about held a candle to what she had been through in the last twenty-four hours, but she didn't want to get into that with her sister right now. "I had to go to Fairbanks yesterday, and I happened to run into Jace Angeles. You remember him?"

"Lindsay's brother? Of course I do."

"Well, he was riding the train to his family's back-country cabin today, and I decided to ride along to Anchorage instead of taking the plane. It's a beautiful trip."

Nicole huffed. "I can't believe you're on a scenic train ride when I'm—" Nicole paused, and Hannah heard what sounded like a paper rustling. In a calmer voice, Nicole asked, "When will you be back in Anchorage?"

"The train is supposed to arrive about seven this evening."

"Come to my house as soon as you get in, okay? Hannah, this is important. Bring all the things you got at that Linacott auction. Everything. I, uh, have something to show you."

"Is it about the marquetry box you got at the auction?"

"N-not really."

"Because I was wondering who you sold it to. Do you know the customer's name?"

"I don't." Nicole's response was immediate.

"Well, how about his description?" Hannah continued. "I don't suppose it was a tall blond man?"

"I—I have to go. Just bring those things immediately once you get back to town."

"Fine."

"And bring that antique you got from Grandpa, too. I'll see you this evening." The call ended.

Hannah slowly returned the phone to her pocket. "That was strange. Nicole wants me to bring the stuff I got at the auction directly to her house when I arrive in Anchorage. I wonder if she thinks the stained-glass lampshade I got might be a real Tiffany. I haven't had a chance to look closely." She turned to Jace, preparing to tell him about the rest of the conversation, but he was staring at her. "What?"

"You just told Nicole you were on the train."

"Yeah. So?"

"Who else did you tell?"

"My manager, Sue Ann. Why?"

"Don't you see? Those guys in the white truck knew what time you would be heading for the airport this morning. Someone is feeding them information."

"It wasn't Nicole. I didn't even tell her I was going to Fairbanks." She paused. "Unless my mom told her. Which, yeah, she probably did."

"Did you give your mom your itinerary?"

"Yes. But Nicole is my sister. We might compete over antiques, but she's not going to help someone rob me."

Jace tapped his chin. "Maybe her phone line is bugged, or her email got hacked, or something."

"That sounds a little paranoid," Hannah said. "Although—"

"What?"

"She kept saying to bring all the stuff I won at the Linacott auction to her house as soon as I arrive in Anchorage, but just before she hung up, she mentioned I should bring the antique I got from Grandpa."

"What's odd about that?"

"I don't have anything of Grandpa's. My grandmother loved antiques, but Grandpa didn't. He was always shaking his head over all her 'clutter.' He used to say that he'd had enough hand-me-downs growing up, and that the only sentimental thing he owned was the memorial flag from his dad's funeral."

"Your great-grandfather was a veteran?"

"Yes, and he was in the Alaska Territorial Police here before statehood. He died before I was born, and my grandpa died when I was about eight. My mother has my great-grandpa's flag down in Arizona, so I can't imagine why Nicole would ask me to bring it. She hung up before I could ask what she meant."

"That is odd." Jace thought for a minute. "What about your manager? Could she be feeding someone information?"

"I trust Sue Ann completely. She's not just my employee, she's my friend. She would never purposely do anything to put me in danger." Hannah's eyes widened. "Except—"

"What?"

"That text. Sue Ann said Tiff told the blond man who asked for me that I was on the train and wouldn't be back until this evening. What if—"

"You can't get off the train in Anchorage," Jace declared. "It's too dangerous."

Hannah drew back. "What do you mean I can't get off in Anchorage? What other choice do I have? There are no other stops between here and there."

"There are whistle stops. The train will stop to let me off near the cabin." He gazed directly into her eyes. "Come with me."

"To the cabin? That's ridiculous. I'll call the Anchorage police before I get off the train and ask them to meet me at the station."

"Okay, and then what? Someone grabs you in the parking lot, or breaks into your house? They know you have the globe, and they need to get it before you have a chance to lock it up. You should come with me."

Hannah shook her head. "I can't just disappear for a week until the next train. People would be frantic."

Jace thought for a moment. "Okay, get off the train with me, we wait a couple of days for everything to settle down, and we can ride the snow machine to Pika, the nearest town on the road system. That's what I was planning to do next Friday. A driver is scheduled to pick me up there and take me to Anchorage for the grand opening. I can call and they'll send a driver for you."

"But I promised Nicole I would come to her house this evening."

"Text her and say you can't make it. Make some excuse, like you're not feeling well. Don't tell her where you're going. Seriously, Hannah, your life could be at stake."

She thought about it. "You'll take me to Pika day after tomorrow?"

"I promise."

Still, she hesitated. "If I don't show up for work tomorrow, Sue Ann will have the state troopers looking for me."

"Text her too. Just don't give out any information as to where you are. Quickly, before you lose the signal."

Hannah closed her eyes and breathed a prayer, "Lord, guide me." On the one hand, Nicole had sounded upset, and Hannah should be there for her sister. But on the other, what if the blond man was waiting to rob her at the train station? When she opened her eyes, there was Jace, his face filled with concern. Jace, who had been keeping her safe since the moment they reunited.

"All right," she told him. "I'll text them now."

SIX

The train pulled to a stop where Jace had requested. There were several cabins in this roadless area, accessible only by train or snow machine in the winter, float plane or ATV in the summer. The train employees were quite accustomed to flag stops. Jace had half-expected a last-minute argument from Hannah about leaving the train, but here she was, standing beside Scout while Jace took a quick inventory of all his gear. Once everything had been unloaded, the train whistled and pulled away.

Fortunately, the temperature here was a good twenty-five degrees warmer than it had been in Fairbanks. Hannah wandered a few steps away. Next to the track, where the plow had pushed the snow, it was hard-packed and she could walk easily, but once she had gotten a few feet away, her boots sank into the snow up to her knees. "The snow is so soft, I'm post-holing."

She looked back at Jace. "How far to the cabin? I can't remember."

"Almost three miles, but don't worry. I thought ahead." He opened one of the backpacks and pulled out a pair of oyster-colored weatherproof ski pants. He handed them to her, along with one of the ski bags. "Hope everything fits."

"You brought me skis?"

"And boots. Size seven, right?"

Hannah studied him with narrowed eyes. "So this is why you had to drop by the store. You've been planning to take me with you to the cabin all along."

"Yes," he admitted. "Ever since that ambush this morning, I've been worried that they know more than they should about your schedule, and I didn't want you going to the train station alone."

She put her hands on her hips. "I don't know whether to be angry or flattered. What were you going to do if I refused to get off the train with you?"

"I was going to go with you to Anchorage," he admitted.

"But the train only runs once a week. You would have had to give up your whole vacation to do that."

"Correct." He grinned. "So it's good that you agreed to come to the cabin. Right?"

After a long, tense moment, a slow smile crept

onto her face. "I guess. But you have to stop doing this, making decisions without consulting me. I'm a grown woman. I don't need a babysitter anymore."

"Agreed." She was all grown up all right, and she'd matured into a lovely, capable woman. He still felt the need to protect her, but not the same way as when she and Lindsay were kids, acting on all of Lindsay's wild schemes.

While Jace loaded the ice chest, duffel, and backpacks onto the sled, Hannah pulled off one snow boot and pulled the leg of the ski pants up over her sweats. Then she stuck her foot back into the boot and repeated the procedure with the other leg. Jace was impressed with her ability to stand on one foot while pulling on clothes. She unzipped the ski bag and tried on the back-country ski boots he'd brought for her. "Perfect fit. I can't believe you remember what shoe size I wear."

"Whenever we went on a family ski or to the cabin, I was always the one in charge of gathering ski equipment for the whole group," he explained as he laced up his own ski boots. Then he confessed, "And I happened to see the size inside your boot when you left it by the door last night."

"Tricky." She grasped her ski poles in one hand, dropped the skis on the snow, and stabbed the toes of the boots into the bindings. "I'd challenge you to a race, but I can't remember the way to the cabin."

"It wouldn't be fair anyway." Jace stepped onto his skis and attached a belt around his waist to which he fastened the towrope of the sled. "Because I'll be pulling the luggage."

Hannah smirked. "I know."

Jace laughed as he skied forward, dragging the sled behind him. Hannah followed, and Scout brought up the rear, smart enough to let them break trail instead of bounding through the snow on his own. Jace set a good pace up the first hill, but Hannah had no trouble keeping up. Less than thirty minutes later, the cabin's chimney pipe appeared. As they climbed the last hill, the rest of the cabin came into view, and Jace experienced a familiar mix of anticipation and nostalgia. So many great family moments had happened here.

Beside the door hung a welcome sign Lindsay had painted dark blue with white lettering and pale blue forget-me-not flowers scattered across the bottom. It had been a Mother's Day gift, probably Mom's favorite gift ever. She had painted the rocking chair beside the door to match, the blue creating a pop of color against the white snow and brown wood of the cabin.

Jace paused for a moment to savor the sight. It

looked like more than a foot of snow had fallen since he was last here, with some clinging to the moose antlers on the gable over the porch. The moose had shed them right in front of the cabin one January, shaking off his huge antlers like a couple of annoying insects while Jace's whole family watched from the front window. Hannah had been there, too. She and Lindsay had been the ones to insist that the moose's "gift" needed to go on the cabin.

Hannah pulled up beside him at the top of the hill and caught her breath. "It still looks great. You must take good care of it."

"I try. I put a new coat of sealer on the logs last summer." He pushed forward. "Come on. Let's get a fire going." They glided down the hill and stepped out of their skis. Hannah hung both pairs on sets of pegs on the porch wall while Jace transferred all the baggage from the sled to the porch and unlocked the front door. Inside, they shed their ski boots and set them to dry on the mat beside the door.

Jace glanced around the room, noticing the battered pine kitchen table, the faded cushions on the chairs, and the worn rug on the floor, and realized while he'd been taking care of the outside of the cabin, he'd allowed the interior to get a bit shabby. But when he looked over at Hannah, she was looking up at the heavy timbers that supported the roof. Her gaze traveled down the walls and all around the front room. "I love this place. It feels so solid, like it will still be here in a hundred years, safe and snug."

Jace felt it, too, every time he came to the cabin. "Sanctuary." He crossed to the stove and, using the firewood and kindling he'd left at the ready last time he was here, made short work of building the fire. Meanwhile, without being asked, Hannah began wiping down the kitchen surfaces. Once they were clean, she unpacked the freeze-dried and other nonperishable foods and arranged them on the shelves, leaving Jace free to shovel a path to the woodshed.

He finished just before the sun reached the horizon. When he stepped inside carrying a load of logs, the scent of chilis, cumin, and stewing meat greeted him at the door. Scout followed him inside, holding his head high and sniffing the air. Hannah stood at the kitchen counter, chopping an onion. Two large cans of hominy sat nearby. "I assumed the pork cubes and hominy were for posole. Hope I didn't overstep."

"No, of course not." He'd planned on making do with canned stew tonight because he'd figured with all the chores, he wouldn't have time to cook the posole until tomorrow, but this was even better. "Smells great."

"I hope it tastes good. Your mom never measured the seasonings, just cooked by feel, so I'm not sure I have them right. The pork needs to cook another fifteen minutes or so before I add the hominy and other ingredients."

"Good. That gives you time to come outside and see the show."

"What show?" Hannah was already grabbing her coat and stepping into her snow boots.

"You'll see." Jace rested a hand on her back and urged her through the door ahead of him and Scout.

As soon as she stepped outside, Hannah's mouth dropped open. "Wow."

Jace grinned. This was exactly the reaction he'd hoped for. The wind this morning must have stirred ice particles into the air, because the sun was a brilliant orange, reflecting off the low clouds and painting the surface of the snow. The light touched Hannah's face, warming her skin until it almost seemed to glow, too, as she stared in wonder at the sunset. Jace had the strongest urge to touch that lovely face, to see if her skin was as soft and warm as it looked. Instead, he reached down to ruffle Scout's ears.

"The earth is full of the goodness of the Lord," Hannah whispered, and Jace recognized it as part of a Psalm his dad liked to quote. She continued to watch until the sun had dropped below the horizon and the orange clouds faded to peach. Then she turned to Jace. "Thank you."

"For what?"

"For getting me to stop for the sunset." She spread her arms, taking in the whole view. "It's been too long since I took the time to appreciate the everyday miracles."

Everyday miracles. He liked that. "You mean like sunsets, and snowflakes, and the smell of good food cooking?"

"Yes, exactly."

"I know what you mean. When you run your own business, it seems like there are never enough hours in the day. But Scout here is good about reminding me to take a break, and spending time at the cabin is even better." He brushed snow off the sturdy porch railing and rested his hand there. "Spending time here always reminds me to give thanks for all I have, and for the privilege of living here in the midst of all this beauty."

"Yes." Hannah shook her head slowly. "Here it is March, and I just realized that today was the first time since New Year's Day that I've skied outside. Seems like it's easier to work out on my ski machine in the basement in the morning before I head to work. And that's just wrong." She drew in a lungful of crisp air and let it out again. "Of course, in two days, I'll have to get to Anchorage and figure out what to do about this globe and the people after it, not to mention dealing with Nicole and whatever had her so agitated. Here in the cabin, trouble seems so far away."

"Maybe we should keep it there." Jace touched her arm. "What if, for tonight and tomorrow, we just enjoy the cabin and forget about all that other stuff?" Not that he wouldn't be constantly turning it over in his mind, but Hannah needed a break. Needed to believe in the sanctuary of the cabin. In the sanctuary of God's love.

Hannah ran a hand over Scout's head and smiled. "I love that idea. Let's do it."

After breakfast the next morning, Hannah cleared the table while Jace poured a kettle of hot water into the dishpan. He went outside to refill the bucket with snow and returned to put it on the stove to melt. While he was working on that, Hannah washed their plates and silverware and stacked them in the dish drainer beside the sink. Without a word, Jace grabbed a dish towel and began drying.

It was almost eerie how well they worked together. Hannah supposed it was just because Jace's mom had taught them the chores that came with a backcountry cabin with no plumbing or electricity, but Hannah didn't remember it all running so smoothly when they were kids.

There was the usual grumping and arguing about whose job it was to fetch the wood or sweep the floor. Lindsay would usually come up with some creative reason why it was always Jace's turn, but her parents never let her get away with it. Hannah had never complained about chores—she was just grateful to be included in the Angeles family outings.

She scrubbed the skillet, rinsed it, and handed it to Jace, who wiped it out and set it on the stove to finish drying. He poured kibble into Scout's bowl and set it on the floor. Scout gulped it down as though he hadn't eaten in a month, his wagging tail creating a draft that sent a paper towel drifting from the countertop to the floor. Dodging the tail, Hannah picked up the towel and set it in the kindling bucket. Nothing was wasted at the cabin.

Jace hung the now-dry skillet on its assigned peg and the dish towel on a bar to dry. He picked up a box from the kitchen shelf. "What are these doing here?"

"What are they?" Hannah asked.

"Darts." He opened the box to show her. "I guess I cleaned them last time I was here and forgot to put them away." He carried the box to the cabinet on the living room door that housed the dartboard. He opened the doors, exposing the board, stepped back a few feet, and threw his first dart. Bullseye. Two more darts followed, sticking to the board right beside the first dart.

He pulled his darts from the board and looked at Hannah. "Your turn."

She shook her head. "I haven't thrown a dart in years."

"It's like riding a bicycle," Jace assured her. "Come try it."

Hannah came to stand next to him. She'd never been good at this. She picked up one of the darts Jace offered and threw it. It missed the board entirely, sticking into the door instead.

Jace grinned. "That one didn't count." He handed her another dart. "Here, hold it like this." He put his fingers over hers, adjusting her grip, but the feel of his touch was so distracting, she couldn't seem to concentrate on what he was trying to tell her. Her face grew warm.

"Okay, go," he said.

Hannah let the dart fly. This time it hit the outermost ring.

"Better. One more try." He handed her the last dart and Hannah threw it before he could start fiddling with her grip again.

This time the dart hit three circles out from the middle. Jace nodded approvingly. "There you go. You're getting the hang of it now." He pulled out the darts and looked at her. "Your cheeks are pink. I can damp down the fire if you want," he offered.

"It's fine," Hannah replied quickly. Knowing Jace had seen her blushing only made her blush more, but if Jace noticed, he was kind enough not to comment.

"What do you want to do today?" he asked, as he returned the darts to the box and stashed the box in the cabinet.

"You do whatever you had planned," Hannah told him. "I've disrupted your life enough."

"I was going to give Scout some practice in avalanche search work."

Hannah waved a hand at the shelves under the dartboard stocked with books, games, and puzzles. "Go ahead. I can entertain myself."

"Well, actually," Jace said, "the training would go better with two people. I'd planned on hiding his toy, but if he can search out a hidden person, all the better. If you're up for it."

"Sounds great." Maybe she could repay Jace, at least in a small way, for all he'd done for her. "I would love to play the role of avalanche victim for Scout."

He grinned. "All right then. Let's get ready." He pulled an Angeles Adventure shopping bag from the backpack and handed it to her. "I threw in a few more warm layers for you."

"Thank you!" Hannah retreated to her assigned bedroom and opened the bag. Inside she found a new set of pale lavender thermal underwear, the really soft kind made from bamboo, plus wool socks, a fleece zip-neck pullover, and a pair of insulated ski bibs, heavier than the snow pants he'd given her yesterday. She quickly pulled on all the layers. So thoughtful. She knew if she offered to pay, Jace would refuse. Nevertheless, she made a mental note to send him a check for all the clothes and food once she got back to Anchorage.

When she returned to the living room, Jace and Scout were already there. Scout was dancing at the door, eager to go. Jace handed Hannah a red bandanna. "Here, put this against your skin. Scout will use it later to track you."

Hannah tucked it inside her top and packed one of the water bottles Jace had already filled into her daypack, along with the globe. She stepped into her snow boots. "All set."

They went outside. The sun glittered on the snow, and Hannah realized she'd left her sunglasses in the rental car. As if reading her mind, Jace pulled two pairs of shades from his backpack and handed one to her. He pulled a squeaky toy from his pocket and threw it. "Scout, fetch!"

The dog galloped after the toy. Hannah chuckled. "Training looks a whole lot like playing."

"Yeah, it's basically a game. We'll start with fetch and work our way to hide-and-seek."

Scout came running back with the toy and deposited it into Jace's hand, tail lashing so hard it was going in a circle. Jace threw it two or three more times, working their way into the woods as he went. The snow wasn't as deep here under the trees, and they were able to walk without sinking up to their knees. The next time Scout returned the toy, Jace commanded him to sit and stay, and then handed the toy to Lindsay. "Do you still have that bandana?"

"Right here." She pulled it from under her top and handed it to Jace.

"Great. Take the squeaky toy with you and find a place to hide behind a bush or tree somewhere. Once you're hidden, I'll send Scout to find you."

"How far should I go?" she asked.

"Not too far the first time, but far enough that Scout can't see where you went from here." He looked at his watch. "I'll give a two-minute head start. Go."

Lindsay trotted away down a game trail through the trees, checking out possible hiding places as she went and mentally counting off the seconds. When she figured her two minutes were just about up, she backtracked for a bit and crouched behind a snow-covered boulder about six feet off the trail, still clutching the squeaky toy. She'd left tracks, of course, but that was unavoidable. A raven in the tree above her gave her a scolding for disturbing his solitude. She held her finger to her lips and whispered. "Shh, don't give me away." The raven gave another squawk and flew to a different tree, still making grumbling noises.

Soon, she heard Jace in the distance giving the command to "Find." A short time later, bushes rustled as Scout made his way along the trail. Jace's footsteps followed. As they drew closer, she caught a snuffling sound and the occasional sneeze. Scout trotted right past the boulder without pausing, but suddenly he stopped, sniffed the air and turned, spotting her. His ears pricked and his tail wagged. Two bounds later, he had knocked her down and was lying on her legs, holding the squeaky toy in his mouth.

"Oof." Hannah laughed at the dog. "If you're going to act like a lap dog, you might want to cut back on those between-meal treats."

Jace ran up. "Good boy. Release." He threw a different toy, and Scout dropped the first one to chase after it. Jace offered Hannah a hand. "Sorry about that. I forgot to warn you. Scout has been trained that when he finds someone in the snow, he's supposed to crawl up next to them or lay on top of them to keep them warm until help arrives. Unfortunately, he's concluded that if they're not prone, he's supposed to knock them down. Are you okay?"

"I'm fine. Next time I hide, I'll know what to expect." She took his hand and let him pull her to her feet. For a moment, their faces were only inches apart. Within kissing distance. Now where did that thought come from?

Jace's gaze went to her eyes and dropped to her mouth. Was he thinking of kisses too? Or was that just a scrap of fantasy left over from her schoolgirl crush? He paused for an instant, and then he took a step back. Hannah had probably imagined the whole thing.

Scout returned, and Jace threw the toy once again. "I need to break him from knocking people down, but I don't know how, without discouraging him from seeking. I've decided to let the professional trainer handle it when she takes over. Are you up for another round, or have you had enough?"

"Oh, I'm just getting started," Hannah replied. Scout was already back with the toy, and Hannah reached down to ruffle his ears. "Right, Scout?"

The dog dropped his toy and stared at Jace, head cocked and ears pricked, waiting for his next assignment.

"All right then," Jace said. "Let's keep practicing."

SEVEN

That evening, Jace carried in the Dutch oven with the leftover posole from the porch where they'd stored it overnight, and set it on the wood-stove to heat. "This may take a while," he told Hannah. "It's partly frozen."

That comment sparked a memory for Hannah. "Ooh, you know what would be good with it?"

Jace groaned. "You're not going to try to bake, are you?"

Hannah laughed. She couldn't count the times she and Lindsay had attempted brown-ies, or coffee cake, or bread in the Dutch oven on the woodstove. They'd had the occasional success, meaning the result was more-or-less edible, but most of their experiments had been either charred to a crisp or raw in the middle. Sometimes both. Still, it had never discouraged them from trying, and she was pretty sure she remembered the recipe for corn bread. "Do you have cornmeal, flour, and baking powder?"

Despite his skepticism, Jace checked the metal-lined box where his mom kept her staples safe from mice and other would-be invaders. "We have masa harina for tortillas. Powdered milk. Sugar. I don't see flour, but we have pancake mix."

"That will work, and it already has baking powder in it. How about eggs?"

"We ate all the eggs for breakfast." He dug around a little more. "Well, there is a pouch here of freeze-dried eggs with cheese and jalapenos."

"Perfect. I saw butter in the ice chest." Hannah lifted one of the iron skillets from its peg on the wall, added a chuck of butter, and set it on the stove to melt. She set the next larger skillet on the stove beside it.

Jace watched, a bemused expression on his face while Hannah found a mixing bowl and combined the pancake mix, corn flour, powdered milk, and dried eggs. She picked up the skillet with an oven mitt, tilted it to coat the bottom with melted butter, and poured the rest of the butter into the bowl of dry ingredients. Next, she added water and a squirt of honey, stirring just until the dry ingredients were moistened. The batter sizzled when she poured it into the hot skillet. She returned it to the stovetop and set the larger empty skillet that had been preheating on top as a lid. "There. It should be ready in about twenty minutes."

"If you say so." Jace set bowls and spoons on the table and hung a lantern on the hook above.

"Oh, ye of little faith." Hannah added bread plates and butter knives.

Jace chuckled.

Seventeen minutes later, a hint of smoke had Hannah rushing to remove the corn bread from the heat. She lifted the upper skillet to check her results. The baking powder in the pancake mix must have worked okay, because the corn bread rose just like it was supposed to, but when she ran a spatula underneath to check the bottom, a solid black layer greeted her. She sighed. "It's ruined."

Jace looked over her shoulder. "Maybe not. We could cut off the burned part." Using an oven mitt, he transferred the stew to a trivet on the table.

"You don't have to eat it to spare my feelings."

"Let's try it." Jace cut the corn bread into wedges, severed the burned layer, and gave them each a serving. They sat down at the table, and Jace bowed his head. "Lord, we thank You for this day, for all the progress Scout made in his training today. Bless this food, especially the corn bread Hannah prepared, and if You so please, transform it into something edible, just as You did the water into wine."

Hannah chuckled. "Amen."

Jace spread some butter on his corn bread and took a bite. "It's not bad."

"Yeah, right," Hannah said skeptically. She tried a little taste. "Hey, it really isn't."

"The hint of cheese and jalapeño from the egg mix really jazzes it up," Jace said. "If the stove weren't quite so hot, I think it would have been perfect. Lindsay would be proud."

Hannah stopped eating to look at him. It was one of the few times either of them had mentioned Lindsay.

Jace gave Hannah a gentle smile. "It's okay to talk about her, you know. I'm sure you've been thinking about her. I know I have."

Hannah nodded. "I have. It's just—after everything that happened, I didn't want to do anything to hurt you more."

"It doesn't hurt me to talk about Lindsay." He paused. "Well, it hurts a little bit, but it hurts just as much not to talk about her, you know?"

"I do know," Hannah assured him. "I think about her, a lot. Just last week, these two kids came into the store, and one of them was wearing a horned helmet—"

"Oh, wow." Jace laughed. "I'd forgotten all about Lindsay's Viking phase. When she braided her hair and wore that silly helmet everywhere she went. Mom couldn't even get her to take it off for church. She was, what, seven years old?"

"Eight. We were in Ms. Engels's Sunday school class." Hannah blinked back tears. "Oh, Jace, I miss her. I'm so sorry. If I hadn't lied to your mother about where Lindsay was—"

Jace cut her off. "We all wish we'd handled things differently. Myself included."

Hannah frowned. "You weren't even living at home. You were in the dorm, going to summer school at UAF. None of it was your fault."

"I wouldn't say that." Jace sucked in a breath and blew it out. "You know she was out past curfew drinking with some kids in the woods the weekend before that, right?"

"What? No." Come to think of it, the weekend before Lindsay's accident, Hannah and her mom had driven to Anchorage to spend time with Dad and Nicole. "But that doesn't make any sense. If Lindsay was out past curfew, especially if she'd been drinking, your parents would have grounded her for a decade." The Angeleses were loving but strict parents. Like most teens, Lindsay had rebelled on occasion, especially after she turned eighteen, but her parents told her that if she expected them to pay for her college, she needed to follow their rules. Hannah always sympathized when Lindsay got in trouble, although she'd privately thought the rules weren't that unreasonable. She shook her head.

"No way would they have allowed her to spend the night with me that night."

"They didn't know about it. The friend she'd ridden with ditched her, and she needed a ride home, so she called me. I picked her up and dropped her a block away from home. She'd left the window in her room open, and she sneaked inside without our parents finding out. But the next day after she sobered up, I really came down hard on her. I told her I wasn't covering for her again, that next time I'd wake up the folks and let her face the consequences." He huffed out a breath. "If I hadn't been so judgmental, maybe she would have called me again instead of riding with someone who'd been drinking."

"Or if I'd gone with her to the party, I could have watched over her." Hannah stood up and walked over to the window. She stared outside at the expanse of snow gleaming in the moonlight. "I felt terrible that night. And at the hospital, your parents were so upset, and I—" A sob stole her voice.

Jace came up behind her and put his arms around her. "I felt bad, too. But when it came down to it, the guy chose to drink and drive, and Lindsay chose to ride with him."

"She didn't deserve to die," Hannah protested.

"No, she didn't. But I don't believe she would want us to keep beating ourselves up over what we did and what we didn't do. God forgives, and I think Lindsay would as well."

Hannah turned within the circle of his arms. "Oh, Jace. I miss her so much." Tears poured from her eyes. He pulled her close against his chest and stroked her hair. Hannah put her arms around his waist and held on, as though he was the only thing keeping her from being swept out to a sea of loss and misery. Maybe he was. Hannah felt, rather than heard, the single sob that rattled Jace's chest. She looked up to see answering tears in his eyes.

"I miss her, too," Jace whispered. "But I know she's with the Lord now. And someday, we'll all be together again."

"Yes." Lindsay might have made mistakes, but her faith had never wavered. "I know that's true."

Suddenly Jace grinned. "I'll bet in heaven, no one ever burns the corn bread."

Hannah's tears turned to laughter, especially when Jace added, "But if anyone could do it, it's Lindsay."

The next morning, Hannah dressed and packed her few belongings into her daypack and the Angeles Adventure Store shopping bag. She and Jace had agreed to spend the morning working with Scout again, and then Jace would take her on the snow machine to the closest village.

Pika was a tiny town, but it was on the road system. From there, they figured Hannah would be able to arrange a ride to Anchorage.

Jace's suggestion to forget her troubles for a day had been a good one, but now she needed to be making plans, figuring out how to keep herself and the globe safe, as well as how to appease her sister since she'd backed out of their meeting with nothing more than a text reading:

Can't make it this evening. Not feeling well. Talk later.

But her thoughts kept returning to the conversation with Jace the evening before. To Lindsay.

She washed her face and started to comb her hair, but several teeth snapped off the cheap comb she'd picked up at the box store. That was annoying. She opened the drawer below the washbasin to see if she could find a replacement. Lindsay's purple hairbrush lay right on top, next to a couple of rhinestone-encrusted hair clips. Tucked beside them, for some reason, were some painted rocks. She, Lindsay, and Lindsay's mom, Judy, had painted them on a trip to the cabin the week after high school graduation. They'd even roped Jace and Lindsay's dad, Russell, into the project.

They'd had so much fun that day, gathering

the rocks at the bend of the creek while they watched the antics of a family of river otters who had taken up residence on the far bank. They'd even seen a moose swim across the stream not too far downriver and a fox trotting by. Lindsay had declared that the creek was her favorite spot in the whole world. Later, they'd brought the stones back to the cabin to paint.

Hannah took the rocks from the drawer and spread them out on the countertop. Hers were painted with flowers, mostly daisies and fireweed. Judy's rocks were heavy on mountains and rainbows. Jace's rock was simple, just a brown line with green down-swept branches, forming a spruce tree. Russell's was a moose, although he'd smudged the antlers and Lindsay had teased him that it looked more like a stegosaurus.

Lindsay, who had the most artistic talent of the group, had done several animal paintings based on the shape of the rocks. A sleeping red fox like the one they'd seen that day curled around one rock, and a mallard swam across another, the natural rings in the rock looking like water. Hannah turned over the last rock to see a bald eagle, painted in amazing detail, soaring against a blue sky.

She could hear Jace adding logs to the woodstove. "Jace, can you come in here for a minute?" she called.

He stepped inside the doorway. "What's up?"

She pointed to the rocks. "Remember these?"

Jace stepped closer. "Oh, yeah. You gathered them down at the creek that one day."

"Look at this one." She handed him the eagle rock. "Remember how Lindsay said it reminded her of a Bible verse?"

"'But they that wait upon the Lord shall renew their strength; they shall mount up with wings of eagles,'" he quoted without hesitation.

"That's the one. Hannah loved that spot where we gathered the rocks, at the river bend. I was thinking we could take this rock and leave it there, as sort of a memorial."

"That's a great idea."

Hannah hesitated. The rocks had been in a drawer, after all. "You don't think your parents would mind?"

"They would love that idea, and so would Lindsay. Let's do it."

Once they'd eaten breakfast, fed the dog, and banked the stove, they strapped on their skis and headed out. A cold breeze nipped at their noses, but the sunshine on their backs made up for it. The wind calmed as they arrived at the creek, now completely frozen across except for a space about a foot wide in the center where the water rushed too fast to be caught by the cold. An ancient spruce grew tall and thick on the bank. Birch branches, heavy with snow, bowed over the murmuring water. It looked completely different now than it did in the summer when they'd gathered the stones, but every bit as beautiful. Hannah knew Lindsay had loved this spot in all seasons.

The spruce branches had deflected the season's snow away from its trunk, forming a well about three feet deep. Hannah stepped out of her skis and took the eagle rock from her daypack. She carried it to the spruce tree and set it between two roots at the bottom of the tree well.

She returned to Jace and they stood without talking for several minutes, just listening to the birdsong. To the water whooshing past the ice in the middle of the frozen creek. To the wind rustling the tree branches. It was the voice of God's creation, and Lindsay had loved it more than anything. Hannah reached for Jace's hand. "Would you like to pray?"

"I would." He gave her hand a squeeze. "Our Father, we come to You today with heavy hearts. We miss Lindsay. But we also come with thankfulness for those years she was in our lives. Her joyful spirit was a gift to us, and to everyone around her, and we're grateful. Hannah and I are grateful, too, for this opportunity to share this moment of remembrance. In Jesus's name we pray. Amen."

"Amen," Hannah whispered and opened her eyes. "Oh, Jace, look!" On the far bank, a fox, looking dapper with his white shirtfront and furry red coat, watched them curiously. "There was a fox there that day when we gathered the rocks. It couldn't be the same one, could it?"

"No, but it could certainly be his great-something grandson. The cycle of life continues."

"Beautiful." She turned to Jace. "Thank you for coming with me today. Somehow, I feel…" She groped for the word.

"Peaceful?" Jace suggested.

"Yes. And lighter. As though a burden I've been carrying has been lifted." She looked into his eyes, a window to the gentle spirit inside him.

"I feel that way, too." He pulled her into a hug.

It felt so good, standing there on the riverbank with their arms around each other, warm and safe, as if they'd shut out all the dangers and complications and worries of the outside world. Here it was just the two of them, drinking in the beauty of their surroundings and remembering someone they had both loved. Hannah felt like she could stay there in Jace's arms forever, but Scout chose that instant to notice the fox across the river and let out a barrage of barking. The fox fled, Jace turned to calm the dog, and the special moment was over. But the warmth of the hug stayed with Hannah.

A sudden gust of wind shook the branches and a splat of snow fell to the ground, barely missing them. Jace looked at the sky. "We'd better get back to the cabin. The forecast called for high winds tonight and a couple inches of snow tomorrow morning, but it looks like the front is arriving early." Another gust confirmed his theory.

The wind continued to pick up strength as they skied toward the cabin. When they reached the point where the trail converged with their tracks leading in from the train, Jace stopped, frowning.

"What's wrong?" Hannah asked, but then she spotted it too. The crosshatched tracks of a snow machine covered their own tracks leading to the cabin, although wind-driven snow was already beginning to erase them. "Do you think…" Hannah trailed off, unwilling to put her fears into words.

"It could be the neighbors." Jace's words were optimistic, but he still looked worried. "Eli Jones and his family have a cabin about five miles from here and they sometimes stop by to say hello. Although, when I talked to Eli a month ago, he said something about a Hawaiian cruise."

He examined the tracks more closely. "Whoever it was, they've come and gone. The tracks go both ways." But he stared toward the cabin, that worry line between his eyebrows. Scout, sensing his mood, pressed against his leg, and Jace absentmindedly reached down to stroke his head.

They continued on until they crested the hill, and the cabin came into sight. "Oh, no," Hannah whispered. The blue chair on the porch had been knocked over, and the door stood open. The welcome sign lay in broken pieces on the snow in front of the porch. The chaos from Fairbanks had somehow followed them. The cabin was no longer a sanctuary.

Hannah's first impulse was to hurry forward, to see what damage they had done to the inside of the cabin, but Jace put out a hand to stop her from moving out of the protection of the woods. She looked at him. "You think they might have left someone behind," she guessed.

He nodded. "It's possible. Let's circle around and approach the cabin from the back, just in case."

They did just that, crouching behind the woodshed, but after watching the cabin for almost thirty minutes, they saw no sign of movement other than loose snow and broken twigs blowing across the clearing. "I'm going closer." Jace had to raise his voice to be heard over the wind, even though he was only a few inches away. "You keep Scout here."

Hannah nodded and grasped the dog's collar. Jace skied up to the cabin and then stepped out of his skis to creep closer to one of the bedroom windows. He looked inside, then moved to the next window and did the same. He circled the cabin, moving out of Hannah's field of vision. After what seemed like forever, the high window from the loft opened and Jace leaned out. "They're gone. Come on in."

Hannah released Scout and the two of them circled to the front porch and stepped inside. She gasped. It looked as though the cabin had been through a major earthquake. All the books and games on the shelves were dumped on the floor. The ice chest stood open, and all the kitchen gear was strewn about. Even Scout's dog food had been emptied from the bag. Jace climbed down the ladder from the loft. "Same story up there. They had to be looking for the globe."

"I had it with me." Hannah pulled off her backpack and took out the object of their search. "They might be back, and they won't be happy if the globe isn't here. Maybe instead of dropping me off at Pika, you'd better come with me to Anchorage."

Jace's mouth was set in a grim line. "I think that's a good idea."

Hannah picked up some of the plates on the floor. "Not broken, fortunately."

Jace laid a hand on her arm. "Don't worry about that. I'll clean up when I get back, once this is all behind us. You get your stuff together, and I'll do the same. We need to head out."

"Okay." He was right, although she hated leaving him with this mess. "Jace?"

He turned back, "Yes?"

"I'm sorry I dragged you into this."

He gave a little smile. "I'm not. Come on, get your things and dress warm. We'll be in Anchorage by nightfall, and we can turn this all over to the police."

EIGHT

Jace closed the ice chest and moved it to the front porch. Better to let the contents freeze in case he didn't make it back to the cabin in the next few days. It all depended on what happened once he got Hannah safely to Anchorage and they talked to the police. Hopefully, Hannah could get that globe tucked away in a safe deposit box, or in police evidence, or somewhere secure. But even then, how would she get the word out to would-be robbers that she wasn't carrying it around anymore? And what was so special about that globe, anyway?

He went back inside and scaled the ladder to the loft. After shoving one of the beds there to the side, he located the ring embedded in one of the floorboards. Fortunately, whoever had searched the house hadn't discovered it. He pulled up on the ring and the section of the floor lifted out, revealing a compartment about fourteen inches square and ten inches deep. Inside was a metal box. He pulled out the box, turned the four numbers to the proper combination, and opened the lid. Inside, a portable GPS lay beside Dad's .45 Winchester Magnum pistol.

Too bad there wasn't a satellite phone there as well to call the state troopers. When their store first began carrying the phones, Jace had suggested they get one for the cabin, but Dad had nixed the idea. He said the whole point of the cabin was to get away from work and everyday stresses, and if he carried a satellite phone, work would just follow him. He made a good point, but Jace could have really used that phone right now. He tucked the pistol into his backpack, along with a box of ammunition and the GPS. Dad kept the gun at the cabin as protection from bears, but whoever was after Hannah might be even more dangerous than an angry grizzly.

He shrugged on the backpack and climbed down the ladder. Scout waited at the bottom. Hannah was at the door, about to step into her snow boots. "Wait." Jace ducked into his parents' bedroom and returned carrying a pile of puffy outerwear. He tossed one of the jumpsuits to Hannah. "You can borrow my mom's snowmobile suit and gloves."

"Thanks." Hannah pulled the suit up over her clothes. The temperatures outside weren't that cold, but the wind chill on a snow machine could bring on frostbite in a hurry if the passengers weren't bundled up.

They gathered up their things and stepped outside, into the gale. After Jace locked the cabin door, they had to bend forward to make their way through the blowing snow to the shed. Ordinarily, Jace would never go out in conditions like this, but with the portable GPS unit, he was confident he could find the way to Pika. His first inkling of trouble came when he noticed extra footprints in the snow near the shed. The wind must have blown them clear between the cabin and the shed, but on the leeward side, a few tracks remained, and they hadn't been made by him or Hannah. When they reached the door, he wasn't surprised to find that someone had used bolt cutters to remove the padlock.

Hannah leaned around him to peer at the mangled lock lying in the snow. "This doesn't look good."

"No." When he unlatched the door, a gust of wind jerked it from his hand and slammed it against the wall. He and Hannah stepped inside to find the hoods open on both snow machines. As his eyes adjusted to the relative gloom inside the shed, he was able to see parts and pieces scattered everywhere.

"Oh, no!" Hannah surveyed the wreckage. "Now what?"

Jace picked up the nearest part, which happened to be a carburetor. "I guess I try to put it back together. Looks like that auto shop class I took in high school might come in handy."

"What if you can't fix it?" she asked. "Whoever did this must intend to come back, or they wouldn't have bothered to disable the snow machines."

"You're right. And the train doesn't run again until Saturday." He considered the options, which were few. "If I can't fix this, we'll have to ski out. We should be able to make it to Pika in under two days."

Hannah picked up a stray bolt that had rolled under the edge of a shelving unit against the wall. "This looks hopeless. Maybe we should start skiing now."

Another gust shook the shed. "We're almost in whiteout conditions," Jace said, "but the wind is supposed to die down tonight. Chances are, since they think we're stranded, they'll wait for the storm to pass before they come back. If we leave first thing tomorrow morning, we should be able to make it to Pika the day after tomorrow. If we left now, that would mean two overnights, and I'm not thrilled with the idea of tent camping in this weather."

"Good point. I don't think we could even set

up a tent in this gale. Okay, I don't know much about mechanics, but how can I help?"

Jace considered the best way to attack the problem. "Let's collect all the parts and lay them out on the floor in some kind of order."

Hannah nodded. "I'll go inside and get some lanterns, so we can shut the door and get out of the wind while we work."

"Thanks."

Forty-five minutes later, after they had collected all the parts, it was clear the snow machines weren't going anywhere. The intruders had torn the wires from the distributor caps and broken the spark plugs. For all Jace knew, they could have contaminated the fuel in the tank as well. He couldn't detect any odor other than gas, but then if they'd just added water, he wouldn't. He huffed out a breath. "I suppose we should be grateful that they didn't set the shed on fire."

Hannah shook her head as she gazed down at the assorted parts. "I'm just sorry that your reward for helping me is to have your snow machines destroyed."

"I don't think they're destroyed," Jace said. "I just can't fix them without getting more parts. Once this is behind us, I'll get someone to come over from Pika and haul these to a shop for a complete overhaul. They're due for a tune-up anyway." He put a finger under her chin and tipped up her face so that their eyes met. "And none of this is your fault, so don't start feeling guilty."

She gave a rueful smile. "It's a long-standing habit."

"Well, it's time to change that. And speaking of change, looks like we're going to Plan B. So let's take these lanterns back to the cabin and dig out our equipment for snow camping." Saying the words reminded him of the one and only time his parents had taken them all camping in the winter. Dad had planned on doing all the cooking on a camp stove, but Lindsay and Hannah insisted it wasn't a real camping trip if they didn't roast marshmallows over a fire.

When the wet wood they gathered refused to burn, they had sacrificed most of the marshmallows to use as a fire-starter, leaving only one apiece to roast. When Lindsay's last marshmallow fell into the fire, Hannah offered hers. The two girls had ended up sharing a s'more, the same way they'd shared almost everything. Jace grinned. "We'd better carry plenty of fuel for the camp stove, because I don't have marshmallows this time."

Hannah laughed. "I remember that trip. Best s'more ever. You know, I haven't eaten a s'more in years."

"Me neither. Next time, we'll have to bring a

bag of marshmallows." The words slipped out before Jace remembered that Hannah didn't live in Fairbanks anymore. He wouldn't be sharing marshmallows or anything else with her once he'd seen her safely home. And that thought saddened him more than he wanted to admit.

Busy gathering the lanterns, Hannah didn't seem to notice his slip. They stepped outside, where Jace pushed a screwdriver into the hasp to hold the shed door closed until he could return with a new padlock. Bracing themselves against the wind, they made their way to the cabin.

It felt so familiar, being here with Hannah, as if the thirteen years of absence had just fallen away and their relationship had simply picked up where it left off. But no, that wasn't quite true, he realized. Back then, she'd been almost another sister, but now there was something more humming between them. When he'd held her in his arms at the river, looking into her face, he'd wanted nothing more than to kiss away those tears, to bring back that wonderful smile.

Once they'd gotten out of their jackets and boots, Scout went to lean against Hannah's leg. She stroked his head. Jace wasn't the only one Hannah had charmed. She crossed to the stove. "How about if I build a fire and heat up that leftover posole while you get the equipment together?"

"Sounds like a plan." With the two of them working together, it didn't take long to clean up the mess the intruders had left and gather up the camping equipment. Soon, they were sitting at the table, enjoying bowls of hot soup and cold corn bread. Outside the wind still howled, but inside the cabin they were warm and cozy. Tomorrow night might be a different story.

Once they'd finished supper and washed dishes, Hannah took the globe from her backpack and held it close to the light of the lantern in the center of the table. "There has to be more to this than a simple ornament. Maybe there's something special about the design that makes it worth a whole lot more than Karas's other globes."

Jace leaned closer. "You mentioned puzzle boxes."

Hannah nodded. "Peter Morozov, the expert in Fairbanks, said Dimitri Karas made a few, but the ones he described were cubes about eight inches square. But since each art piece he made was custom, there's no reason he couldn't have designed a ball puzzle." She ran a finger over the smooth wood in the Indian Ocean. "But if he did, I can't imagine how it would work. Everything fits together so tightly."

"May I see?"

Hannah passed the globe to Jace. She was right—there didn't seem to be any gaps. Except...was that a crack in the center of the equator, or simply a slight groove? He looked closely at the minuscule strips of dark wood circling the globe. "There's a tiny space here. It's hard to see, because there's dark wood underneath, but I think the two hemispheres might be separate pieces. Can you feel it?"

Hannah ran a fingernail over the line. "Yes! It's shallow, but I can feel a little depression."

"Without more light, it's hard to tell, but if it is a puzzle box, that raises another question. Is it the puzzle box itself the guys in the white truck are after, or is there something inside?"

Hannah ran her fingers over the surface. "I suppose we could smash it," she said slowly. "Although I hate to destroy that beautiful work."

Jace shook his head. "Only as a last resort. If it is a puzzle box, there has to be someone who can tell you how it works. And you could always have it x-rayed to find out if there's something inside. But first, we need to get it and you to a safe place."

"Agreed. And since we're planning to head out before dawn tomorrow, I suppose we'd better get some sleep." Hannah rewrapped the globe and returned it to her backpack. "Thank you, Jace, for everything you've done."

"I can't say I've done much. I thought you'd be safe here, but they found you."

"But you've been with me, protecting me." She leaned toward him, close enough for him to catch a whiff of her scent, clean and natural, like rain. "And you can't imagine how much it means to me that you've forgiven me for my part in Lindsay's accident."

"And you've forgiven me for mine. We both loved Lindsay, and we miss her, but she would want us to be happy."

"Yes, she would." She pressed a kiss to Jace's cheek. "Good night, Jace."

"Good night, Hannah." He waited until she'd disappeared into her room before running his finger over the cheek she'd kissed. It still felt warm. What would a real kiss with Hannah be like? He suspected it just might be life changing. Was that good or bad? If anyone had asked him last week, he would have said he liked his life just the way it was. Now, he wasn't so sure.

But he couldn't let himself be distracted by what-ifs and future possibilities. He needed to concentrate on the here and now, on standing between Hannah and the danger that kept following her. Whatever came, Jace would keep her safe. Somehow.

The wind died down about midnight, as Hannah could attest, since she'd spent most of the night tossing and turning. She should have been sleeping, gathering strength for the grueling trek to come, but her swirling thoughts kept her awake. It wasn't memories of the strange men in the white truck, of Jim White grabbing her arm at Peter Morozov's place, or of the ransacked cabin that disturbed her sleep. Rather, it was thoughts of Jace, of the concern on his face when he'd insisted she come to the cabin with him. Of his warm, woodsy scent when he'd held her in his arms. Of the feel of rough stubble on his cheek when she'd kissed him good-night. Maybe she shouldn't have done that, but she couldn't bring herself to regret it.

When she faced herself in the mirror the next morning, she noticed dark circles under her eyes, but since her makeup bag had been inside her suitcase and she hadn't picked up more at the store, there wasn't a lot she could do about it other than splash some cold water on her face. She dressed in the weatherproof ski pants Jace had provided, knowing the insulated bibs would be too warm once they started skiing.

Jace was already up, working at the wood-stove. He looked up and smiled. "Good morning. Coffee in five. Bacon and pancakes in ten." If he'd had any trouble sleeping, it didn't show. In fact, he seemed energized, as though they were about to head out on a grand adventure rather than fleeing danger. But when he turned to pick up a skillet, she spotted the tension in his shoulders. He was putting on a brave face for her. The least she could do was return the favor.

"Coffee sounds great." Scout rushed to greet her, and she ran a hand over his soft fur. "Good boy. Are you ready to go snow camping, Scout? Are you?" She couldn't help but smile as the dog wagged so hard he wiggled all over. She set her backpack next to the other gear and went to the window, cupping her hands around her face to better see into the dark. "It's snowing."

"I know." Jace stirred the batter in a red ceramic bowl. "But that's good. It will cover our tracks."

"True." There was still a little breeze stirring the snowflakes, but nothing like yesterday's wind. "You have the route mapped out?"

"Yes." He nodded toward the portable GPS on the table. "It's kind of a roundabout path, but I'm taking us through the woods as much as I can. We'll be harder to spot, and the trails are too narrow for snow machines." He poured coffee into a cup and handed it to her.

"Thanks." She helped herself to some sugar from the bowl on the table, enjoying the little conveniences while she could. Tomorrow's breakfast would be camp coffee and freeze-dried eggs, at best.

It was still dark when they headed out, their

headlamps spotlighting the dancing snowflakes falling from the sky. Jace led the way, dragging a sledload of gear behind him. Hannah and Scout followed. They all wore packs, including Scout, who carried his own kibble, rolled mat, and collapsible bowls for food and water. Once they were in the woods, the snowfall slowed, and all Hannah had to do was follow Jace's tracks, through the forest, beside the streams, and up and down the hills. She considered herself fit—after all, she worked out almost every day at the gym or on her ski machine at home—but she was puffing like a steam locomotive as they crested a particularly steep hill.

Jace stopped there, pulled out a water bottle, and handed it to her. "You're doing great." Frost clung to his eyebrows and two-day beard, but he was barely breathing hard.

"Thanks." Hannah gulped some water. "It's been a while since I did any backcountry skiing."

"It's different than groomed trails, for sure." He accepted the bottle back and took a drink. "Hear that?"

Hannah raised her head and listened, but the falling snow dampened even the usual forest sounds. "I don't hear anything."

He smiled. "Exactly. You never get that on city trails."

Hannah looked eastward. Trees blocked their

view of the horizon, but the overcast sky was beginning to grow lighter. In a nearby tree, a chickadee called, "Dee-dee-dee." Another called back, and a few seconds later a mixed flock of chickadees, nuthatches, and sparrows darted overhead only to alight in a tree on the other side of the clearing. The last of the breezes had died away, and the big feathery snowflakes seemed to dance in the air before settling on Scout's fur.

It had been too long since Hannah had taken a moment to really appreciate the beauty of a snowy day. She smiled at Jace. "You're right."

Scout came up beside him and opened his mouth. Jace squirted in some water and adjusted the dog's pack. "Guess we'd better keep moving. Are you ready?"

"Ready," Hannah assured him, and she kept assuring him on every break throughout the day, even as her leg muscles threatened a mutiny.

Finally, he stopped in a level clearing next to a boulder the size of a school bus, no doubt deposited by some glacier long ago. "How does this look for a camp spot?"

"Perfect." Although in all honesty, she would have said the same if he'd suggested they camp in the middle of a five-diamond ski run in avalanche country if it meant she could stop moving for a while.

But she hadn't earned her rest yet. First, they

had to stomp down the snow in the clearing, then put up the tent, and finally, ferry all their gear inside. It was another hour before Hannah leaned back against one of the gear bags with a deep sigh.

"Sore?" Jace asked, as he hung a lantern from a hook on the domed ceiling of the tent and arranged his foam mat and sleeping bag.

"I will be. Right now I'm too tired to feel anything."

"Here." He reached into a duffel and handed her a small bottle of ibuprofen and a water bottle. "Take two of these." Once she'd swallowed the pills, he pulled off her boot.

"What are—?" she started to ask, but when he began kneading the ball of her foot, she smiled and closed her eyes. "That feels amazing."

He chuckled and kept massaging the sore muscles of her foot and calf, then switched to her other leg. By the time he'd finished, Hannah was all but asleep. Jace pulled the insulated ski bibs from a pack and handed them to her. "Better put these on and keep those muscles warm. I'll get started on supper," he added as he dug out a camp stove and a couple of instant meals.

"I'll help," Hannah offered, but Jace waved her offer away.

"I can do it. You rest. Remember to hydrate." He slipped out of the tent and Hannah took another swig of water and changed into the heavy pants. Fifteen minutes later, Jace was back, carrying the foil pouches and two sporks. "Chicken and rice or lasagna?"

"They both sound great. You choose."

He chuckled. "We're talking freeze-dried food here. It won't be great, but we need the fuel. Here, you take the lasagna. You used to love Italian food."

"I still do. Thanks." After a heartfelt prayer of gratitude for safe travel and food, she opened the pouch and took a bite. Maybe it wouldn't be gourmet food under other circumstances, but tonight the dried cheeses and saucy noodles tasted better than any restaurant meal in recent memory. Scout, who was eating his kibble, stopped and shot a hopeful glance her way. She paused, a sporkful of noodles halfway to her mouth.

"Don't," Jace said. "He knows he's not supposed to beg."

"Sorry, Scout. I've been overruled." She put the bite into her mouth and Scout went back to his kibble. In no time, she'd finished the whole meal. Jace collected the empty pouches, rolled them up, and stuffed them in the duffel. She could almost hear his dad's voice reminding them, "Pack it in, pack it out. Leave no trace." Russell always carried an extra bag to pick up after any other campers who hadn't been as considerate. Hannah had learned so much tagging along with Jace and Lindsay's family.

Jace ducked out of the tent again, and when he returned, he was juggling two cups and two water bottles.

"What's this?" Hannah asked as she took the cups from him.

"Hot chocolate. And a hot water bottle to warm up the foot of your sleeping bag."

"Nice." Once he'd slipped the bottles inside the sleeping bags, she returned his cup and took a sip from her own. "Yum! Room service, massage, a hot water bottle… Do you have a mint for my pillow, too?"

He snapped his fingers. "I knew I forgot something."

She laughed. "I don't know why you're being so good to me. All I've done is drag you into a hot mess and gotten your cabin ransacked. You probably wish you'd taken Scout to the dog park instead of to the Ice Sculpture Championships that day."

"Not at all." He met her gaze, and she could read the sincerity in his eyes. "I'm glad I was there, and I'm glad I'm here, with you."

Their eyes held, and Hannah found herself wondering, not for the first time, what it would be like to kiss Jace. Not just a kiss on the cheek, like last night, but a real kiss. She gave herself a mental shake. This wasn't the time for her old teenage crush to come rushing back. There was too much history there. Even if they'd forgiven each other for their own part in Lindsay's accident, it was still there, between them, and she wasn't sure his parents would be so generous with their forgiveness.

Besides, there were practical reasons she shouldn't kiss Jace. They had no future. He was CEO of Angeles Adventure Stores, based in Fairbanks, and she had invested so much of herself in the store in Anchorage. He was just helping her until she could get the globe to the authorities and be safe. Then he would be going home, and they might never see each other again.

Reluctantly, she pulled herself away from his gaze and reached inside her backpack for the globe, which she unwrapped. The workmanship she'd been so appreciative of now seemed to mock her. Was it just an ornament, or was it more? "What secrets are you hiding?" she whispered.

"May I?" Jace asked. She handed it to him, and he examined it for several minutes. "You know, each of the continents has a tiny line around it. Oh, look! If I put my finger in the very center of Antarctica and push, it sinks a little. So does Australia."

"What! Let me see."

Hannah scooted closer and he demonstrated that he could push each continent like a button. When he removed his finger, each one popped back into place. "It has to be a puzzle box. There's no other reason for moving parts and springs."

"You're right. But how does it open?"

"I don't know." He tried a few more spots. "All the continents seem to be buttons, and so do the North Pole and the compass rose, but they don't do anything, at least by themselves. If this is a puzzle box, I assume we would need to press them in a certain order, like a combination lock."

"A combination!" Hannah exclaimed. "That might be what was on the card."

"What card?"

"Remember the photo I showed you of the box Nicole won at auction? There was an index card inside, with letters and numbers. Let me find it." Hannah pulled up the photo on her phone, enlarged the part with the card, and read, "N, S CW 30: E CCW 45: CR."

Jace looked at the photo. "Okay, N, S, and E could be north, south, and east, but what is CW? Something west?"

Hannah tilted her head. "And what is east on a globe, anyway?"

"I suppose it would be the farthest point from the prime meridian, one hundred eighty

degrees longitude. The international date line."
He pointed to one of the silver longitudinal lines
in the center of the Pacific Ocean. "Here."

"But there are no continents on that line until
you get to Antarctica. No land at all, except—"
she leaned closer "—the Alaskan Aleutian Islands. Look, does it seem like that island right
beside the line is a little darker than the others?"

"Maybe. It's hard to see in this light, and it's
too small to push."

"Just a sec." Hannah checked inside her jacket
where she usually kept a couple of small safety
pins. She unpinned one, opened it, and handed
it to Jace. "Try pushing on it."

He tried it. "It moves!"

"So, maybe N is the North Pole. S is Antarctica. E is that island. We just need to figure out
CR, CW, and CCW. And the numbers."

"The numbers would probably be longitude.
Thirty degrees is either here…" He pointed to a
spot in Africa. "Or here." He moved his finger
to the Pacific Ocean. "Depending on whether
it's east or west."

"Maybe that's what the W means," Hannah
suggested.

"Okay, but why the C with it? CW is written
together."

"Center West? Is there a button at thirty degrees on the equator?"

Jace tried pushing the pin into that area. It slipped into the depression in the center of the equator line but didn't seem to activate any sort of button. Instead, it just slid along the line. "No button. I think the equator might be where the box opens up once we get the combination right."

"Hmm. Like it unscrews?" Hannah gasped. "What if CW means clockwise, and CCW means counterclockwise?"

Jace gently tried to turn the two hemispheres in opposite directions. "It doesn't move."

"You'd need to do the combination first. Try pushing the North Pole, then Antarctica, then turn it clockwise."

"Clockwise from top or bottom?"

"I don't know. Try both."

He did. "No, still can't move it."

"Hmm." She stared at the photo. "Wait. What if you hold the N and S buttons down while you turn clockwise?"

"Let's see." It took him a few moments to figure out how to position his hands so that he could hold it all at once, but when he tried it, the hemispheres shifted. "Eureka!"

"Hurray! Okay, stop once you've turned thirty degrees. Now hold the Aleutian button with the pin and turn counterclockwise forty-five degrees."

Jace did it. "Okay. Now what?"

Hannah frowned. "It just says CR."

"CR," Jace repeated and stopped to think. "Compass rose?"

"Try it!"

He pushed on the center of the compass rose, and with a click, the globe fell into two halves, exposing a white foam ball with a seam in the center. "Yes!"

Hannah blinked. "I can't believe it worked."

"Now let's see what someone was hiding in here." Jace removed the ball and handed it to Hannah.

Holding her breath, she pulled the two pieces of foam apart. Inside was a transparent plastic box, about two inches square, holding a coin.

"What is it?" Jace asked.

"It looks like a gold coin."

"Nice. What's gold worth now? About two thousand dollars an ounce?"

"Yes, but I'm sure this is worth a lot more. I'm no coin expert, but it looks old. Too bad Nicole isn't here. She knows way more about coins than I do." Hannah picked up the box and examined the coin inside. It featured a woman's profile in classic Greek style, wearing what looked like a tiara with the word "Liberty" written on it. Stars lined the border of the coin, with the date at the bottom. "It was minted in 1854."

"So, really old."

"Yes, and probably rare. Between 1933 and 1974, it was unlawful to hold gold in the United States. When the law passed, everyone was supposed to deliver their gold coins to the government, who melted them down, so most of the gold coins minted before that are gone." Hannah turned the coin over to reveal an eagle with a shield on its chest. One foot held a clutch of arrows, and the other a branch. Around the rim were the words "United States of America" and "Five D." She pointed to the letter S underneath the eagle. "This means it's from the San Francisco mint."

"Is that important?"

"It can be. If a certain mint only produced a limited number of a certain coin, that drives up the value." She handed Jace the coin in its box. "And that pretty much exhausts my expertise on the subject of collectible coins."

"It's more than I knew." Jace opened the lid and examined the coin. "Five dollars, huh?"

"Well, five dollars was worth a lot more in 1854."

"Feels about as heavy as two quarters. It's hard to believe it's really worth all that much, even if it is made of gold."

"Hard to say. At the Linacott auction where I got the chest that was holding the globe, they were auctioning off some coins. I didn't pay that much attention since I'm not a coin collector, but I remember that a four-dollar gold piece, which apparently is rare, went for more than twenty thousand dollars."

He snapped the box closed and handed it back to her. "In that case, you'd better hang on to it. It's too much responsibility for me. I might accidentally put it into a vending machine."

She laughed. "Not a big concern at the moment." She returned the coin to the foam ball and tucked it inside one hemisphere of the wooden globe. She set the other hemisphere on top. It only took a slight twist to put it back together again. She started to tuck the globe inside her backpack but paused. "You don't suppose..." She trailed off, staring at the globe.

"What?" Jace asked.

Hannah looked up. "You remember when we were talking about that gold coin robbery at the airport? I was in eighth grade, so it would have been seventeen years ago."

"The one where the five coins were missing, the courier was drugged, and later an airport employee found dead? Yeah, I remember."

"Well, what if this is one of those coins?"

Jace raised his eyebrows. "Wait, I thought we decided Candace Linacott was mixed up in the walrus ivory scandal, not the gold coins. Besides, you said she was cleared."

"I said she wasn't charged. What if she was the mastermind behind both? If she managed to get away with robbing a courier, she wouldn't balk at smuggling ivory."

"That's a big leap."

Hannah sighed. "You're right. I have absolutely no evidence that she had anything to do with the gold coin robbery. But if she did, that would explain some things."

"Like what?"

"Like why these men are so determined to get their hands on this globe. According to my history teacher, the coins stolen in that robbery were incredibly rare. Do you remember the value of the stolen coins?"

"No idea. Fifty thousand dollars?" he guessed.

Hannah shook her head. "I don't remember the exact figure," she said, "but it was more than a million."

NINE

Jace's eyes flew open. Still dark. He wasn't sure if whatever had woken him was part of a dream or real, so he lay still, listening. After a few seconds, Scout gave a low growl. Jace could just make out the shape of the dog with his nose pressed against the door of the tent. Had whomever ransacked the cabin managed to follow their trail despite the wind and snow? Jace pulled on his boots and reached into his backpack to collect his head lamp, his dad's pistol, and the box of ammunition. He loaded the gun. At the click of the bolt engaging, something outside the tent made a scuffling noise.

Scout reacted by pressing against the tent fabric with a whine, but Jace pushed him into the down position and whispered "stay." Scout reluctantly obeyed. Slowly and silently, Jace unzipped the door of the tent. A visual sweep of the area revealed nothing except that in the hours they had been sleeping, the skies had cleared.

The new-fallen snow glistened in the light of a full moon. He crept out of the tent and spotted a set of tracks, the kind made by some four-footed creature, crossing close to the tent and then heading into the woods. He blew out a breath and allowed his body to relax.

"What's going on?" Hannah whispered from the door of the tent.

"Nothing important. An animal passed by." He turned on his headlamp to get a better look at the tracks and identify them, but something green flashed in the woods. He trained his light in that direction, and a pair of emerald animal eyes reflected the light back at him. The animal took a step out of the woods, and Jace recognized the tufted ears and flat face. "A lynx."

"I see it," Hannah answered, softly. Scout tried to squeeze past her, but she grabbed the dog's collar. "Oh, no you don't." In a flash, the big cat disappeared into the woods.

Jace turned to Hannah. "You okay?"

"Of course." Hannah put her hand to her chest. "I just thought for a second—"

"Me, too. But it's okay. We're safe."

Hannah pushed the dog back before crawling out the door and zipping it closed. "The snow stopped." She stood and looked around. "It's so pretty."

"Yeah, it is." The temperature had dropped

with the clearing skies, but all around them moonlight reflected off the new fallen snow, bathing everything in a silvery light.

Hannah looked toward a particularly tall spruce, its limbs drooping gracefully under their load of snow. Her eyes followed the trunk upward. "Oh, Jace. Look!"

An owl perched at the top of the tree, staring down at them. Scout whimpered. Jace unzipped the tent and let the dog out, convinced the lynx was long gone. He grabbed his sleeping bag, unzipped it, and draped it over Hannah's shoulders.

"Thank you." She flashed him a smile and held out one side of the bag, inviting him in. "Join me?"

"Love to." He pulled the end of the bag over his left shoulder and because it seemed only natural, slipped his right arm around Hannah's waist. She leaned into him, her head on his shoulder. Scout came to sit at their feet.

A million stars twinkled in the blue velvet sky overhead. A few high clouds drifted, painting ever-changing pictures among the stars. A sweep of green appeared for a few seconds and then it was gone. "Northern lights," Hannah whispered.

"Maybe they'll come back," Jace whispered back to her. With Hannah's warm body pressed against his side, Jace felt as though he could stand there forever, watching the sky. They waited, but the northern lights seemed to be over for the time being. Jace was about to suggest they return to the tent when a sudden streak shot through the sky.

Hannah gasped. "A shooting star! Oh, make a wish, Jace."

But, other than Hannah's safety, Jace couldn't think of anything he wanted in that moment that wasn't already there with him.

Hannah turned toward Jace, moonlight spilling over her lovely face, eyes sparkling like the brightest stars. "With all the streetlights, we can't see the stars like that in Anchorage. I'd forgotten how amazing they are."

He took a moment to study her face. "I'd forgotten how amazing you are."

Her lips parted, and he leaned closer, but just before their lips touched, he hesitated, suddenly unsure. But Hannah slid a hand behind his neck and closed the gap, pressing her lips to his. He tightened his arm around her waist and pulled her even closer. The heat of the kiss seemed to flow through him, warm and wonderful, like nothing he'd ever experienced before. It was like he'd been born to kiss this woman.

After a long moment, he pulled back and paused to look again at Hannah's face, familiar and yet somehow brand-new to him. Was her nose always so perfect, her eyelashes so long, her eyebrows so gracefully arched? He kissed that adorable nose, brushed his lips against her velvety cheek, and couldn't resist a kiss on each eyelid before returning to her mouth.

Her hand went up to cup his jaw. "Jace," she whispered against his lips, and he lost track of the cold, of his surroundings, of everything except for Hannah and the thrill of kissing her. When he finally broke the kiss, she smiled at him. "The lynx, the stars, the kisses—is this really happening or am I dreaming?"

"Let's find out." He leaned in for another kiss.

Wham! A furry missile crashed into them, knocking them to the snow. Scout was lying on Jace's chest, wearing a pleased expression and breathing dog breath into Jace's face. Hannah, sitting on the snow beside him, was laughing so hard tears were running down her face. "You—" she began, but had to gasp for breath before continuing. "You did say find."

"I did." Jace pushed the dog off his chest and sat up. "Buddy, we're going to have a word about your sense of timing."

Hannah grinned and then glanced at her watch. "Speaking of timing, there's not much use going back to bed. The sun will be up in an hour." She stood and offered Jace a hand.

"You're right." Mentally, he shifted gears. This wasn't a date. He was here to protect Hannah, and he shouldn't let himself get distracted. "We have a lot of miles to cover today. We might as well get started." He took her hand and let her haul him to his feet, but he couldn't resist stealing another little kiss before he let go. *Last one*, he promised himself. "I'll get some water boiling for coffee."

Five hours later, the sun had just about reached its zenith for the day. Jace slowed his pace going up a big hill, just enough to give Hannah a rest without it being obvious that's what he was doing. She'd been pushing herself hard, not that he could blame her for being eager to get back to safety, a community…home. He'd thought he was keeping her safe by taking her to the cabin. Instead, here they were, fleeing cross-country for their lives, with no way to contact the authorities. Jace could tell by her ragged breathing that the hours of backcountry skiing were wearing Hannah down.

He was feeling it, too, especially since he was dragging the sled filled with camping equipment. Jace had hoped to be in Pika by noon, but he'd underestimated how much the gear and new snow would slow them down. Now it was looking more like early afternoon. And after they got there, he would still need to call a driver service and wait for a driver to come from Anchorage.

Once they got close to the village, they might be able to pick up a cell phone signal and call ahead, but he doubted it. As he recalled, cell service was pretty iffy, even in the town. He reached the top of the hill and paused to rest.

"Why are…" Hannah sucked in a breath "… we stopping?" She pulled up beside him. Scout, always hoping for a treat, ran up and sat in front of them.

"Snack break. We need calories." He handed Hannah an energy bar and tossed Scout one of the dog treats he always carried in his pocket before helping himself to another bar.

"Oh." Hannah leaned forward with her hands on her knees and closed her eyes while she caught her breath. With her long lashes brushing her rosy cheeks, her face reminded Jace of the angel atop his family's Christmas tree. Once Hannah's breathing had returned to normal, she unwrapped the bar and took a bite. "Chocolate almond. Yum." She swallowed another bite. "How much farther to Pika?"

Jace checked his GPS. "About ten miles, but there are a couple of stiff climbs on the way. And we have to take it slow crossing that area up ahead. It's pretty rugged." As long as they stuck to the trail he'd mapped out, they should be fine, but there were several ravines in the area, and new snow tended to camouflage them.

Hannah finished her bar and stuffed the wrapper into her backpack. "Ready?"

"Not yet." This was their first big descent of the day. He snapped a second cord onto the back of the sled and handed it to Hannah. "Can you hold the sled back so it doesn't run over me on the way down?"

"Of course." Hannah tied the cord around her waist.

Jace pushed off. If he'd been skiing unencumbered, he would have picked a line almost straight down the hill, but with the sled and Hannah in tow, he chose a gentler, more winding route. Hannah followed in his tracks, holding back the sled. They made a good team. Although, after those incredible kisses early this morning, he had a hard time thinking of Hannah as simply a teammate.

What was this between them? A simple attraction fueled by adrenaline and the romance of moonlight, or was it more? Once Hannah had turned over the globe and coin to the police, then what? Did he and Hannah go their separate ways, or—

"Watch for that branch," Hannah called, and he navigated around a stray limb from a nearby currant bush sticking out of the snow just enough to trip an unwary skier. The last thing they needed right now was an injury.

Jace turned his attention to the trail. One thing at a time. He needed to keep his mind on keeping Hannah safe today. Tomorrow would take care of tomorrow.

They made it to the bottom of the hill, and Jace unclipped Hannah from the sled. Scout, who had trotted on ahead, started barking.

"What is it, boy?" Jace called. The dog only barked harder and then took off at a run, away from the main trail. "Scout, no. Come! Come back, now!" he yelled, but he might as well have been whispering for all the good it did. So much for all those hours of obedience training. Scout was still young, and like human teenagers, young dogs sometimes made poor choices. Jace was going to have to go after him.

"Stay here with the stuff," Jace told Hannah as he unclipped the towline from his belt. "I'll be right back." He skied after the dog, who had disappeared down a game trail that veered off from the main trail. Jace had been following for fifteen minutes or so without any glimpse of Scout when he heard another bark, followed by a surprised yip. Jace raced toward the sound and followed the trail around a bushy spruce, only to slide to a stop when he found his way blocked by the back end of a moose.

The moose swung around toward him and Jace ducked behind a nearby birch. Scout stood on the other side of a clearing with his head lowered, occasionally throwing out a nervous bark and probably wishing he'd never started this confrontation. Jace was afraid that yip earlier meant the moose's hoof had landed a blow, most likely a glancing one since Scout was still standing. In between them, a much smaller moose snorted at the dog. Just the situation they didn't need—an agitated mama moose convinced her calf was in danger. "Scout, quiet," Jace commanded, and this time the dog obeyed.

The moose swung her head toward Jace and then toward Scout, trying to decide which was the bigger threat. "It's okay." Jace tried for a soothing voice as he eased farther into the woods, putting distance between himself and the moose. "Nobody wants to hurt your baby."

Scout chose that moment to abandon the standoff and make a run toward Jace and the safety he represented. Unfortunately, the moose interpreted his sudden movement as an attack and lashed out at him. Scout dodged her hoof and ran directly toward Jace, with the mama moose right on his tail. Jace tried to jump out of the way, but his ski caught, and he stumbled backward. A flash of yellow fur streaked past followed by the moose, her bulk catching Jace and knocking him completely out of his skis. He went flying and landed in the snow, but the snow gave way, and he was falling again. He hit something hard, a pain shot from his knee, and then he was rolling in the snow, fruitlessly trying to catch himself. His gloves found nothing but loose snow to grab on to, but finally he came to rest on his back, facing upward. He seemed to be in one of those ravines he'd hoped to avoid.

He sucked in a lungful of air. Okay, he was breathing. So far, so good. Even better, none of his ribs seemed to be broken. No dizziness when he sat up. His knee hurt, but he didn't think it was anything serious. Until he tried to move it and discovered one of his legs was wedged between two rocks.

He tried pulling it toward himself, but the stiff sole of his ski boot was caught on something, and he couldn't seem to wiggle it loose. Lifting the leg from the crack was impossible, because of the angle at which his leg had come to rest.

About ten feet above him, a gap in the snow revealed a patch of sky, quickly blocked by a furry yellow face looking down at him. Scout whined.

"Oh, so now you're concerned about my safety," Jace chided. "I hope the moose have moved on. Stay there, boy. I'll be up in a minute." He tried bracing his free leg against the rock and pushing, but the stuck boot still refused to budge. This was getting ridiculous. Jace was strong and fit, and not seriously injured. There had to be a way to get himself free so that he could climb out of the ravine. He just needed to…or maybe…

Fifteen minutes later, he was forced to accept the truth. He was stuck.

TEN

Hannah took another drink from her water bottle and checked her watch. How long could it possibly take to catch a runaway dog, especially one that was supposedly obedience trained? Was Scout hurt? Maybe he'd come across a porcupine. Or wolves. Or he could have fallen through some thin ice on a creek. Jace could be trying to figure out how to pull him out of the freezing water without falling through the ice himself right now. And he didn't have any gear with him. She'd better take Jace's pack and go look for them.

But before she could even hoist Jace's pack from the sled onto her back, Scout burst out of the woods and galloped in her direction. She was relieved, even when the dog jumped on her and almost knocked her down. "Hi, Scout." She pushed him down until all four feet were on the ground and gave his neck a good rub. "Where's Jace? Did you outrun him?" She looked up the trail, but she didn't see any sign of him approaching. "Jace?" she called.

There was no answer and her fear returned. Was Jace in trouble? Scout sat at her feet, staring up as though he was expecting a command. Come to think of it, the only time the dog ever knocked her down was after he'd been ordered to "find." Maybe Jace sent him back for her.

She opened Jace's backpack, found a sock, and held it under Scout's nose. "Scout, find." The dog immediately raced back down the trail. She pulled Jace's pack onto her back and followed. Fortunately, it was easy to follow Scout's trail in the new snow. Before long, she found where he'd branched off from the main trail into the woods. In the distance, she could hear Scout barking. Maybe he'd found Jace already.

The trail ended in a patch of trampled snow in a clearing. Scout continued to let out a bark every few seconds, but there was still no sign of Jace. Skiing toward the dog, she spotted something bright yellow. As she got closer, she recognized Jace's skis, one of which had been snapped in half. What could have happened to him?

She picked up the skis. "Jace?" she called, and this time, she got an answer.

"Hannah! I'm down here. Be careful, there's a ravine."

Hannah dropped Jace's skis, stepped out of

her bindings and laid down her poles, shrugged out of Jace's heavy pack, and made her way to where Scout was standing. She grabbed onto a sturdy branch and leaned over the edge. Jace lay at the bottom of the ravine, several feet below. Her stomach did a flip, as it always did when she stood on ledges. "Um, hi there."

He chuckled. "Hello. I can't tell you how glad I am to see you. Scout and I had a little run-in with a mama moose, and I wound up here."

"Are you hurt?" She didn't see any blood, but only the upper half of his body was visible from where she was standing.

"Not much," he told her. "Just wrenched my knee a little."

"Can you still climb? I'll get the rope from your pack and throw it down."

Jace shook his head. "Unfortunately, that won't work. I seem to be stuck here."

"Stuck? What do you mean stuck?"

"I mean I can't pull my leg out of this crack between rocks with my ski boot on, and I can't reach to get it off. I'm going to need you to come down here and remove it. The boot, not the leg," he clarified with a grin.

"Down there?" Hannah squeaked.

"Yeah. I know you don't like heights—"

"No, I don't like pistachios. I'm terrified of

heights. Are you absolutely sure you can't get loose?"

"Believe me, I've tried. I'm sorry, Hannah. You know I wouldn't ask you if—"

"No, I know. It's okay." She sucked in a breath. "I can do this." She stood at the edge of the ravine, trying to plot a path down, but her vision blurred, and everything began to swim. She stumbled back away from the edge and reached for a tree trunk to steady herself. There was no way she could do this.

"Tie yourself off to a tree," Jace called. "You can hold onto the rope to help you down."

"Hold on to the rope. Right. I'll do that." She closed her eyes and leaned against the tree, feeling the rough bark against her cheek. "Lord, I can't," she whispered. "I can't make myself go over the edge of that ravine. But Jace is down there, and he needs my help. And I need Yours. So please, Lord, give me courage. Amen." She opened her eyes. Scout stared up at her, waiting for her to act. He'd done his part, and now it was time for her to do hers.

She got the rope from Jace's pack, wrapped it around the big cottonwood she'd been leaning on, and tied it in a square knot. Then she tied another knot, because one couldn't be too careful. "In God, all things are possible," she told herself, as she tied the other end of the rope around her waist.

"In God, all things are possible." She walked to the edge and looked down. Her heart pounded, but this time her vision stayed clear. God was helping.

"There's a ledge about four feet down and six feet to your left," Jace told her. "Try that first. But it's covered with snow so be careful putting your weight down until you're sure it will hold you."

"Okay." Hannah moved to her left. *In God, all things are possible.* She turned her back on the ravine, grabbed the rope in her gloved hands, and sort of slow-motion rappelled down the edge of the ravine, until she reached the ledge. She put down one foot and pushed, but the snow held. The second foot held as well. She looked at the ledge, but she didn't have the nerve to look at the bottom of the ravine.

"You're doing great," Jace told her. "I can't see you from here, but is there a boulder or something behind you where you can climb?"

She took a deep breath and checked. "Yes," she called. It was only about three feet down. *In God, all things are possible.* She sat on the edge of the ledge and eased her right foot down until it rested against something solid. She pushed off the ledge to bring her left foot down, but

her right foot slipped and skidded. She yelped
and grabbed the rope, swinging herself forward
and banging her shoulder against the edge of
the ravine.

"Hannah!" Jace yelled. "Are you okay?"

To her surprise, she was. Her shoulder had
bumped against the rock but didn't hit hard
enough to damage anything. "I'm fine," she assured Jace. She was now directly over another
ledge, and a foot below that, she could see Jace's
black ski boot. Because of the way the wall jut-
ted out, she could no longer see his upper body.
Bracing herself against the wall, she let herself
gingerly down to the ledge, which proved solid.
The boot was now hidden under the ledge. She
removed her gloves and felt around underneath
until her fingertips brushed heavy fabric. "I can
feel your boot."

"That's great. Can you get it off?"

"I think so." She ran her fingers up the boot
until they hit the Velcro strap at the top. It made
a ripping noise as she pulled it apart to expose
the laces. It took a minute to sort out the laces
by feel, but eventually she was able to locate a
lace tip and pull until the bow untied. She tied
the end of one of the laces around her wrist before working the boot loose.

"I can feel that," Jace called. "It's getting
looser."

"Good. I'm pulling on the heel. Can you flex your foot?"

It took some wrestling, but with a final tug, the boot slid off his foot. Hannah lost her balance for a second and almost fell from the ledge, but she managed to grab the rope and catch herself. Good thing she'd tied the boot to her wrist, because otherwise it would have dropped another six feet, and she really, really didn't want to climb down there after it.

Some gravel crunched as Jace flexed his foot and wriggled his leg through the opening. "I got it. I'm free!"

"Thank You, God!"

"Amen." A minute later, Jace's hand appeared past the jutting part of the wall. Slowly, he worked himself around, hugging the wall, until his left socked foot was on the ledge with Hannah. When he put his weight on it to swing his right foot around, a little grimace passed over his face, but a second later, he was standing beside her. As soon as he was secure on the ledge, he pulled her into his arms. "Thank you for saving me," he whispered against her hair.

She wrapped her arms around his waist, accidentally banging the back of his leg with the dangling boot, but he didn't seem to mind. "Anytime."

He leaned back so that she could see his face

and smiled. "I'll try not to let it happen too often. Now, why don't you give me that boot, so that we can get out of here."

"Brilliant idea."

Climbing up was less scary than getting down, especially with Jace to give her a boost from below. Once Hannah was on solid ground, Jace pulled himself up using the rope, although it was clear each time he used his left leg that he was feeling pain in that knee. Scout whined, and Hannah had to hold him back to keep him from rushing Jace while he was teetering on the edge of the ravine. As soon as Jace was clear of the edge, Hannah let go of the dog's collar. Scout rushed to Jace, sniffing him up and down as though to reassure himself that Jace was all in one piece.

Jace ruffled his ears and then ran his hands over the dog's body. Scout winced when Jace's hand reached his ribs. "Yeah, you've got a bruise there, probably where her hoof caught you. It could have been a lot worse. I hope you learned your lesson about chasing moose." He untied the rope and coiled it into a neat bundle. "Well, we didn't expect that delay, but we should still be able to make it to Pika from here in ninety minutes or so." He limped toward the clearing and picked up the ski poles he'd dropped in the fall. "Have you seen my skis?"

"Unfortunately, yes." Hannah held up the broken ski. "How did this happen?"

"Oh, shoot. The moose must have stepped on it when she knocked me into the ravine." He made a face. "It might take a little longer than ninety minutes, after all."

"Guess we'd better get started, then." Hannah pulled on Jace's pack and slung her own skis and poles over her shoulder.

"I can carry that," Jace protested.

Hannah shook her head. "You're doing well to carry yourself. That knee looks painful."

"I just wrenched it a little. It's nothing serious," he claimed, but there was a definite limp with each step as they made their way through the woods. Once they reached the main trail where the snow was deeper, Hannah stepped into her skis, but Jace was forced to walk, post-holing through the snow with each step while they made their way back to the spot where Hannah had left the sled. There was no way he was going to be able to walk ten miles like that.

Jace must have come to the same conclusion. "I should have packed snowshoes, as a backup," he said in a low voice.

Hannah took off the heavy backpack and set it in the sled. "We have plenty of food and fuel. We'll take it slow."

"Or…" Jace opened the backpack and pulled

out the GPS. "I'll set a pin for this location. You just need to follow the route I've set, and once you reach Pika, you can give my location to Search and Rescue."

Hannah stared at him. "You want me to leave you here? Injured? With moose and lynx running around, not to mention whoever ransacked your cabin? No way."

"It's the only way. I'd slow you down too much if—"

"Get on the sled," Hannah demanded.

"What?"

"The sled. It won't be comfortable. You're going to have to hold most of the gear in your lap, but we can make it work. Give me your tow belt."

He hesitated and then slowly unbuckled the wide belt. "Are you sure?"

"I'm sure," Hannah said as she adjusted the size of the belt. Jace wouldn't be here, wouldn't have gotten injured if he weren't trying to help her. Once this was all over, he would probably want to get as far away from her as possible, but she wasn't about to leave him here alone. "It's better if we stick together. You know this trail better than I do. You can help me avoid the ravines."

"Like I've done so well today," he muttered, but he began unloading the gear from the sled.

"Oh, wait. I have an idea." He removed the rope from his backpack. "I can make a harness for Scout, and he can help you pull."

Hannah glanced over at the dog, who was rolling in the snow. Maybe he'd gotten too warm after all that running and adventure. "Are you sure that's a good idea?" If Scout objected to pulling, he might be more hindrance than help.

"I've taken him skijoring. He knows how to behave in a harness."

Hannah considered Jace's idea. If the dog could pull a skier, he should be able to pull a sled. "Okay. Let's try it."

Hannah watched while Jace tied the rope in a series of loops to create a sort of web that went around Scout's neck and across his chest, between his legs, and then back up to come to a vee just above his tail, avoiding the bruised spot on Scout's lower rib cage. He padded the parts around the neck and chest by wrapping a fleece pullover around the rope there and securing it with duct tape, a roll of which any self-respecting Alaskan would never be without. Finally, he tied a loop at the back of the harness, where Hannah would be able to clip the sled's towrope.

"Impressive," Hannah said. She fashioned a second, longer towrope out of rope and extra carabiners from Jace's pack. "Let's get this show on the road."

Jace sat in the sled with the tent bag, the duffel containing their sleeping bags and camping equipment, and Hannah's daypack piled up in his lap. It looked like a miserable ride, but Hannah couldn't think of any way to make him more comfortable.

After adjusting the straps on Jace's pack to fit her, Hannah pulled on the pack and clipped herself and Scout to the sled. "Okay, let's go. She leaned into her skis and pulled forward.

"Mush," Jace called, and Scout leaned into his harness, too. *Less than ten miles to Pika*, Hannah reminded herself. *Easy peasy.*

ELEVEN

Jace shifted the duffel in his lap. Nothing like being carried along on a sled like a piece of luggage to keep a man humble. A verse from Proverbs popped into his head. *A man's pride will bring him low, But the humble in spirit will retain honor.* Well, his honor should remain intact. His position on the sled was hurting his back as well as causing his knee to throb, but he wasn't going to complain. Not when Hannah was towing him and all their gear up a challenging slope.

He'd been afraid she was reaching the end of her endurance before, when he was still dragging all the gear, and yet here she was, chugging along, mile after mile. And that was after facing her fear of heights and climbing down into a ravine to save his life. Hannah Yates was one impressive human being. Scout was helping, making up for his earlier faux pas by leaning into the harness and pulling some of the weight, but Hannah was doing most of the work. When they reached the top of the hill, Jace called for a stop. "You need a rest."

Hannah checked the GPS. "But we've still got four miles to go."

"Ten minutes won't make that much difference, and besides, you can't pull the sled down that hill without someone behind to moderate the speed. I'd run right over you."

She frowned. "Then how can we get you down?"

He'd been thinking about this. "It's a sled, right? We'll let gravity do the work. I'll slide down and meet you at the bottom."

Hannah looked down the steep hill and laughed. "You're just bored and looking for a thrill."

"You got me." He smiled and took out a water bottle. "Better drink and eat while you can. There's one more big climb before we get to town."

While Hannah snacked on some trail mix and Scout ate a dog biscuit, Jace unhooked the sled from its towline and pushed forward with his hands until he was balanced on the edge of the slope. The simple plastic sled had no steering or braking capabilities, but fortunately, the slope appeared clear, with no rocks or trees between him and the flat area at the bottom. It brought back memories of fun times at the university sledding hill back home. Lindsay and Hannah used to love sledding. Lindsay would shriek in mock terror, and Hannah would laugh. Jace had always loved her laugh.

"See you at the bottom," Jace said, but before he could push off, Hannah ran up and gave him a big shove, sending him and the sled flying down the hill. Scout barked, Hannah giggled, and Jace couldn't keep the grin off his face.

The zooming sled hit a bump, which sent Jace and all the gear airborne for a split second, and then hit the snow and picked up speed once again. Momentum carried Jace to the bottom of the hill and on past until another bump, this one on the right side of the sled, raised one edge far enough to send Jace and all the luggage tumbling into the snow. Nothing to do but laugh.

By the time Hannah and Scout made it down the hill, he had everything gathered up and was back on the sled. Hannah reached down to brush some snow off his face. "Having fun?"

"You bet." He grinned. "Want to drag me up for another run? You can ride down with me this time."

Hannah chuckled. "I'll take a rain check on that." After refastening the towlines to herself and Scout, she started off. The trail was mostly a gentle downhill here, which would lead to a small lake, frozen solid this time of year, and then a final climb up to the town itself.

When they reached the lake, Jace turned on his cell phone, but as he'd expected, there was no signal. Hannah didn't even slow, skiing across the pond in a few strokes, and then climbing up the hill. She'd almost reached the summit when she ran out of momentum. She turned sideways and began sidestepping up the hill, still dragging him. Jace couldn't stand it anymore. He rolled out of the sled and stood up.

"What are you doing?" Hannah demanded.

"Helping, I hope." There wasn't much snow deposited on this windy knoll, and Jace managed to limp his way to the hilltop. Hannah still had to pull the gear, but at least not his weight, too. At the trailhead at the top of the hill, a well-beaten path led into town. Pika consisted of a handful of houses, a modest RV campground that was closed in the winter, and a general store/post office with gas pumps out front.

Hannah pulled out her phone and turned it on. "I'm not getting a signal."

Jace checked his. "Me, neither. But we can call the state troopers from the phone in the general store. I know Lucas and Marti, the couple who own this place."

Hannah frowned. "If we call the troopers, that would mean waiting here until they show up, and that could be hours or even tomorrow. Let's go back to Anchorage first and turn over the coin to the police there."

She had a point. "That makes sense, especially since you've already reported the break-in at your store, and they have an open case."

"I'll call my sister to see if she'll pick us up. Assuming, of course, that she's still taking my calls after I said I'd come by her house and then stood her up."

"You texted that you couldn't come."

"Yeah, but then I lost the signal, so I don't know for sure if the text made it. If she did that to me, I'd be furious."

"I'm sure she'll forgive you once she understands the situation. And if she's not available, I can call the car service in Anchorage and hire a driver to come get us." They'd reached the general store. A battered Jeep Wagoneer was parked in front with the tailgate open. Hannah wriggled out of Jace's huge pack and set it on the sled with the other gear, replacing it with her small day-pack. Jace commanded Scout to stay with the gear and then limped up the steps to the porch. He went to hold the door for Hannah, but before he could reach for the knob, the door opened and a man with a gray beard, glasses, and a ball cap stepped out carrying a suitcase, which he tossed into the back of the Jeep.

Lucas followed with another suitcase but dropped it when he spotted them. "Jace, hi!" He gave Jace a one-armed hug and slapped him on the back. "Haven't seen you since Christmas when you and your folks stopped by. Who's this pretty lady?"

"This is Hannah Yates. Hannah, Lucas Sutton. An old family friend."

"Hello, Hannah." Lucas shook her hand and then looked over at the dog and gear they'd left near the porch. "Did you ski in all the way from your cabin?"

"Yeah, we did," Jace said, "and now we need to call for a ride. We can't seem to get a cell signal—"

"I know. It's down again. They need to put in another tower or something." Lucas picked up the suitcase he'd dropped. "You're welcome to use the store phone. Or wait—where are you headed?"

"Anchorage."

"Bill!" Lucas called and carried the suitcase to the Jeep. "This is Jace Angeles and Hannah Yates. They need a ride to Anchorage. You got room for them and the dog?"

"Sure, if they're ready now." Bill, who had closed the tailgate, reopened it. "If you don't mind catching a ride from the Anchorage airport, that is, 'cause I don't have time to drop you anywhere else. I can't miss my flight to Honolulu. I'm meeting my kids and grandkids there."

"The airport is just what we need," Hannah answered. "Thanks."

"All good then." Lucas grabbed Jace's duffel and carried it to the Jeep. "Bill will take good care of you."

Jace loaded the camping gear, ski equipment, and backpack into the Jeep. Lucas frowned when he noticed the limp. "What happened to you?"

"Nothing serious. Wrenched my knee."

"Ouch. You should ice that." Lucas started toward the store. "Let me get you a cold pack."

"If you're coming, come," Bill called out the driver's side window. "I'm already running late."

"I'll ice it when I get there," Jace told Lucas as he urged Scout to jump into the back of the Jeep and got him settled next to the luggage. "Tell Marti I said hello. I'll stop by to visit next time." Jace slammed the tailgate shut.

"Are you sure?' Lucas asked. "Won't take a minute."

"No, I'll be fine. But thanks." Hannah was already in the back seat behind the driver, so Jace climbed into the front passenger seat. Lucas waved as they drove away.

Bill pulled onto the highway. "Sorry to rush you out of there, but you know Lucas and Marti. He would have gone in and asked Marti for ice, and she would insist you need your knee wrapped before you go and spend ten minutes with Lucas discussing which bandage he should use. And then while Lucas wrapped your knee, she would have wanted the whole story of how you got hurt, asked about your family, and caught you up on every mutual acquaintance you have with them. Then she would inspect Lucas's job and decide it wasn't right, and that she'd better take the wrap off and do it again, and that would have reminded Lucas of some long, convoluted story, and next thing you know, I've missed my plane."

Jace laughed. "That's exactly what would have happened."

Bill shook his head. "Salt of the earth, those two, but once they start talking, they just don't stop. How did you hurt your knee, anyway?"

"An unexpected run-in with a moose," Jace told him, deciding to skip the details about falling into the ravine, since Bill seemed to appreciate brevity.

"Oh, yeah? I've had a few of those myself." It turned out Bill didn't mind long, convoluted stories after all, as long as he was the one telling them. He spent most of the two-hour trip into Anchorage entertaining Jace and Hannah with his own adventure-filled encounters with moose and bears. Once he'd run out of tales of his own, he threw in a few secondhand wildlife stories from various friends and relatives.

Meanwhile, every time they passed through someplace with cell service, Hannah's phone would ding and she would tense up. Either her sister was really upset or there was something major going wrong at the store. Jace looked at Hannah with raised eyebrows, silently asking her what was going on, but she shook her head. Either she didn't want to tell Jace about it or didn't want to talk in front of Bill. Not that she could have gotten a word in anyway.

It must have been a warm day in Anchorage because there were puddles in the streets where the snow had melted. As the temperature dropped later, the roads were likely to get slick. It was fully dark by the time they turned onto the road leading into the airport. "Want me to drop you at the terminal before I park?" Bill asked. "Should be able to get a cab there."

"I left my car in long-term parking before I flew to Fairbanks," Hannah told him. "So we'll be fine. We appreciate you letting us tag along."

"My pleasure." Bill turned into the long-term parking lot and found a spot not far from the shuttle stop. "It was nice talking to you."

"Thanks, Bill," Jace said as he unloaded their stuff. "Have a great time in Hawaii."

"Oh, I will." Bill grabbed his two suitcases

and locked the car. "I'll get me some of that guava juice and find a nice chair under a palm tree and feel sorry for you poor suckers back here in the snow and ice." He was still chuckling as he turned a corner and disappeared between two parked cars.

Hannah picked up Jace's backpack and pushed her arms through the straps. "I'll carry that," Jace offered, but she shook her head.

"I've got it. My car is right over there." She pulled a key fob from her own small backpack and pushed a button. The horn beeped and lights flashed on a gray SUV at the end of the row. "How's your knee?"

"A little stiff," he admitted as he picked up the duffel bag. "But it will be fine. What's with all the texts?"

"My sister." She opened the tailgate of her car and set the backpack inside. Scout came to sit beside her, waiting for the command to hop in. Hannah absently ran a hand over his head and then pulled the phone from her pocket and frowned at it. "Something weird is going on."

"How so?" Jace set the duffel beside the pack and turned toward Hannah.

"You remember the day we were on the train? Right after I texted her to say I wasn't feeling well and couldn't come to her house after all, we lost the signal."

"Right."

"Well, it looks like she sent six, no, seven texts right after that demanding that I had to come immediately, even if I was sick. Then she called and left a message. All the messages were telling me to come, but not why. Then nothing for the two days we were at the cabin, but today I'm getting messages again. I didn't want to call her in the car with Bill there, but I'd better do it now. I'll explain about the globe and everything and tell Nicole I'll come to her house as soon as we're done at the police station."

"I'll grab the rest of the stuff while you call." Jace went back for the camping and ski gear and stowed it in the back of Hannah's car. Hannah stood beside the open driver's side door, phone pressed to her ear, not saying anything. Her sister was probably giving her an earful. Jace closed the tailgate and stepped to the side, intending to catch Hannah's eye and see if she needed privacy or support.

But Hannah's face had gone pale, her eyes huge. Something was very wrong. Scout sensed it, too, and went to nudge her hand and whimper. Hannah laid a hand on his head.

"Let me talk to her again," she demanded in a shaky voice. "No, I— All right, I understand. Yes, I have what you want. I'll be right there." She ended the call, and whatever color still remained in her face drained away. She looked like she might faint.

"Hannah." Jace hurried to her and grasped her shoulders.

"Jace," she said, as though she'd forgotten he was there, but then she gave her head a little shake and her features settled into an expression of determination. "Oh, Jace, they're holding Nicole hostage at her house. They want the coin."

TWELVE

Hannah got into the driver's seat and started the engine while Jace loaded Scout into the back seat and then hurried around the car to climb into the passenger side. She drove to the pay station at the edge of the parking lot. Jace pulled a credit card from his wallet and handed it to Hannah, but her hands were shaking so much, she couldn't fit the card into the slot. He leaned across and did it for her. A few seconds later, the bar lifted, and Hannah shot forward.

Jace buckled his seat belt as Hannah streaked through a yellow light, and he gripped the handle on the car door when she swerved off International Airport Road and onto the entry ramp to Minnesota Avenue. Once they'd merged into traffic, he reached into his pocket. "I'll call the police."

"No!" Hannah shot him a wild-eyed look before returning her gaze to the road. "They said no police or they'll kill Nicole."

"O-kay," he replied, slowly. No use pointing out the obvious, that if they were willing to kill Nicole, there was nothing keeping them from killing him and Hannah, too, once they had what they wanted.

Hannah bit her lip as she stared straight ahead. "Look, this isn't your problem. I'll let you out at the traffic light at Old Seward."

"What?" Did she really think he would leave her to deal with these people alone? "No way. I'm coming with you."

"You've already hurt your knee helping me." She flashed him a tortured look. "If you got seriously hurt—"

"Hannah, stop it. You're not to blame for Scout chasing a moose, or for me falling. On the contrary, if you weren't there, I'd still be at the bottom of that ravine. You saved my life—simple as that. Now I want to help you help your sister. So no more talk about dropping me off, okay?"

"Okay," she whispered.

He needed to get her past her panic. "Tell me what we're up against. How many people are there?"

"Only one that I know of. Nicole answered the phone and said she'd been kidnapped, but then a guy took the phone away and said to bring the 'item' to her house immediately. I could hear Nicole in the background, trying to get him to let her talk with me, but he wouldn't put her back on."

She tilted her head, the way she always did when she was thinking. "He must have been holding her since the day we rode the train. That's why she was so insistent I come to her house, and why she mentioned Grandpa's antique—the funeral flag belonging to his father, a territorial policeman. She was trying to tell me to call the police." She slapped her forehead. "Why didn't I get that?"

"Why would you? You had no idea she was in danger," Jace pointed out. He tapped his chin. "If the kidnapping was happening on the same day as those guys in the white truck in Fairbanks were breaking into your rental car, that would mean there are at least three people involved."

Hannah merged onto the Seward Highway and passed a slow-moving minivan. "Then there's the blond guy who keeps coming into the store and asking for me, and Peter Morozov's 'neighbor.' They may be involved, too. And all over a stupid coin." She huffed. "I wish I'd never found that globe."

Jace couldn't disagree, but after all, finding interesting and valuable objects was Hannah's business and she seemed good at it. How could she have known it would put her and her family in such danger?

Hannah took the exit to Rabbit Creek Road. There were no streetlights in this part of town, leaving only Hannah's headlights to cut through the darkness and illuminate the winding road. After following the main road for several miles, she turned off onto a narrow side road with thick forest lining both sides.

Jace wasn't familiar with this part of Anchorage. "Where is Nicole's house, anyway?"

"Way upper hillside. It's on five acres, and like I told you, it has an adventure course out back." Hannah took a curve too fast, and the SUV fishtailed on the slick road before Hannah straightened it out.

"Slow down," Jace said gently. "They won't care if we're a minute late, just that we get there."

"Right." Hannah took her foot off the accelerator. But seconds later, just after they'd passed a mailbox, a loud crack sounded. A ragged hole appeared in the windshield. Simultaneously, the driver's side window exploded into a thousand tiny pebbles of glass. Scout gave a frantic bark.

"They're shooting at us!" Hannah hit the gas.

Jace twisted in his seat to look behind them. Scout had wisely scrambled from the back seat to the floor. A familiar white truck pulled out of the driveway they'd just passed and flashed its lights, signaling them to stop, but Hannah kept driving. Jace could just make out two figures in the truck.

"Looks like your friends from Fairbanks are back," Jace announced.

"Friends don't shoot at friends." Hannah took another curve at a less-than-prudent speed. "Why are they doing this? We're bringing them the coin." She paused. "Unless we've got two separate groups who are trying— Oh, shoot, there's the turn." She hit the brake and skidded onto an even narrower snowy road, but lost control and slid off the shoulder, the passenger side of the car coming to rest against a tree. The engine died.

Jace was still watching behind them. "Flip off your lights!" Hannah did it. A second later, the white truck came around the curve and went on by the turnoff.

"Okay, we've lost them for the moment." He reached across and touched her chin to turn her face toward him, but he saw no sign of blood or bruises. "Are you okay?"

"I'm fine. That bump didn't even set off the airbags." Hannah shook off his hand and restarted the engine, but when she tried to pull forward, the side of the car crunched against the tree and the front right dipped.

Jace rolled down his window and leaned out to see what the trouble was. "Blew out a tire.

Come on. We have to get out of here. It won't take those guys long to figure out where we are." He grabbed his backpack from the seat behind him and pulled out the gun, holster, and ammunition before shimmying out the window onto the snow-covered ground. Meanwhile Scout jumped into the front and followed Hannah out the driver's-side door.

Hannah shrugged into her daypack, where she'd stored the globe. "Nicole's house is on the other side of this hill."

Jace put a hand on her arm. "Are you sure you don't want to call the police?"

"I'm afraid if the kidnapper hears sirens, he'll do something to Nicole. I just want to get there and give him what he wants."

Jace figured they didn't have time to argue about it.

"Let's go." He strapped on the holster and picked a path through the trees, which proved to be more of a challenge than he'd anticipated when a sharp pain zinged from his knee, but he couldn't let that slow him down. Rather than follow the drive, he herded Hannah and Scout upward, into the woods. Hopefully the three of them could disappear into the shadows of the trees and bushes before the pair in the white truck found them. Fortunately, the snow wasn't nearly as deep here in Anchorage as it had been at the cabin. Hannah led the way upward through the forest, guided only by the moonlight reflecting off the snow and bouncing through the woods. Scout stayed at her heels, and Jace hobbled along at the rear.

Between the time Jace spent looking back and the pace his tricky knee allowed him, he was falling behind, but maybe that was for the best. If the pair in the white truck came after them, he might be able to slow them down enough to let Hannah escape and make it to her sister's house, where she could turn over the coin and pray that the kidnapper kept his word.

Scout looked back and whimpered. Hannah turned to look. "Jace? Oh no, you're really hurting, aren't you?" She turned and came back.

"I twisted my bad knee when I jumped down, but I'm okay. Go on ahead."

"Not without you." She slid an arm around his waist and pulled his arm over her shoulder. "Come on, let's climb."

Together they made it to the top of the hill. Hannah pointed to a few tiny points of light flickering through the trees far down the hill. "Those are the nightlights from the steps on Nicole's deck. It's not far now."

Still with his arm on her shoulders, they made their way down the steep hill, slipping and sliding on a few spots, which didn't do his knee any good, but they made it without falling. Jace noticed what looked like a metal ladder next to one of the trees. "What's this?"

"Part of the adventure course," Hannah told him. "We must be on Nicole's property now." They pressed forward. The woods were denser here, and for a moment they lost sight of the lights. Then they came around a bush, Hannah stopped abruptly. "Oh no! I forgot about this part."

They were standing on the edge of a bank. Above them, to the right, moonlight glinted off a frozen waterfall that seemed to feed into a narrow gorge. The bottom of the gorge was lost in shadow but, judging by the faint sound of water trickling through the frozen edges of the creek, it was deep. "Is there a way across?" he asked.

Hannah nodded and silently led him downstream until they turned a corner, and there it was—a bridge, if one could call it that. Three ropes, two about waist high and the other at bank level, stretched across the gorge. "This is the only way across?"

"No. There's a hand-tram." Hannah pointed to a cable about twenty yards downstream that connected two wooden platforms. "Unfortunately, it's controlled from the other side, and this is the only way to get to it."

Jace took stock. A guy with a bad knee, a woman with a fear of heights, and a dog. Behind them: two guys with guns. Ahead: a rope bridge between them and their goal. He blew out a long breath. "If ever there was a time for prayer, it's now."

Hannah could hardly hear Jace's prayer because her heart was pounding in her ears so loudly. She'd been on that hand-tram. Once. And once was more than enough. Hanging above a rushing creek in what was basically an oversize wire milk crate, she'd felt like her heart might give out at any moment. But right now, looking at the rope bridge, she would give anything for the safety of that tram.

"...and lend us strength, Lord. Amen." Jace squeezed her shoulders before releasing her. Hannah opened her eyes. Jace took a limping step toward the bridge.

"What are you doing?" Hannah demanded.

"I'm going to cross the bridge." He hobbled closer. "I'll get the tram on the other side and bring it back for you and Scout."

"That rope bridge? With your knee?" Crossing that rope would require steady steps. If his knee gave out unexpectedly, he could fall to his death. "No way."

"But—"

"I'm doing it." Hannah stepped in front of him and surveyed the ropes.

He reached for her shoulders and turned her around so that she had to look at his face. "Hannah, no. You don't have to do this."

"Yes, I do." She flashed a grin. It wouldn't fool Jace, but it made her feel better. "Look, no offense, but you have a rotten track record for staying out of ravines, and I don't have time to bail you out of another one. I'm going."

He chuckled. "Hey, I blame the moose for that one." Then his expression grew serious, and he searched her face for a long moment as though he was building another argument in his head. Finally, though, he sighed and wrapped his arms around her. "Okay," he whispered, just before his lips touched hers. The kiss was short but full of promise. "You win."

"Lucky me." She turned back to study the bridge. Really? Three ropes? Nicole's ex-husband couldn't have sprung for a few wooden planks across the bottom? And how sound were those ropes anyway? Nicole used to have the course inspected regularly when her stepchildren used it, but they had all moved out of state a couple of years ago. But what choice did Hannah have? If they went back to the road, the guys in the white truck were sure to be there and take the coin. Even if they let her and Jace go, if she showed up at Nicole's house without the coin, Nicole's kidnapper might carry out his threat.

The only solution was to get to the other side of that creek, and the rope bridge was their last chance to do it.

Hannah sucked in a deep breath. With God's help, she had climbed into the ravine to rescue Jace. Climbing on solid rocks was child's play compared to stepping out onto a rope, but she reminded herself, "In God, all things are possible." She put her hands on the upper ropes and tested them. So far, so good. She put her right foot onto the bottom rope. It felt solid. But then came the moment of truth. She took her left foot off the solid ground and stepped onto the rope. The bridge swayed, and for a moment so did her courage. She glanced down, and everything went blurry.

Then she heard Jace's whispered prayer, "Lord, please hold Hannah in the palm of Your hand." Her vision cleared.

She eased forward, not lifting her feet but sliding them along the bottom rope. She kept her gaze determinedly on the far bank, never letting it drift down to the depths below. An eon later, she reached the far bank. She stepped onto solid ground and looked back. On the other side of the creek, Jace gave a fist pump. "Amen," she whispered before hurrying to the hanging hand-tram.

Snow had piled up on the platform around the tram. Fortunately, someone had left a snow shovel in the corner, leaning against the railing. It took Hannah several minutes to clear the snow from the decking so that the tram would be able to slide out. Meanwhile, without the benefit of a shovel, Jace was using his boots and a tree branch to clear the twin platform on the other side of the creek. It took Hannah another minute or two to figure out how the locking mechanism worked, but finally, the tram was operational. She climbed into the hanging tram, grabbed the rope that circulated on a pulley, and pulled. With a loud creak, the tram moved along a foot closer to the edge of the platform. Another two tugs, and it was swinging free above the creek.

Hannah's heart missed a beat. She let go of the rope and grabbed the sides of the tram, willing it to stop swinging. In the silence, she heard voices from the other side of the hill. The white truck guys were back! Jace pulled his gun from its holster and loaded it. She grabbed the rope and started tugging, wincing at the loud creaks that might be leading those guys right to their position.

Four minutes later, the tram was over the other platform. Hannah unlatched the gate, and Jace and Scout piled in. With Jace pulling on the lines, they were back across in half the time. They unloaded from the tram, and Hannah locked it in place. She turned to find Jace staring up at the hill across the creek. Something, or someone, was moving through the trees near the top.

Jace limped to the rope bridge as fast as his injured knee could carry him, pulled a knife from his pocket, and began sawing at the bottom rope on the bridge. Hannah unzipped the outer pocket of her own pack, but then she remembered that she'd removed her pocketknife before flying. She watched Jace work, willing the rope to break. A few seconds later, it snapped, falling away into the creek, and he started on the second rope.

Crack! A shot rang out and something ricocheted off a boulder just behind Jace. Scout barked. Hannah grabbed Jace's hand and tugged. "Leave the ropes. We have to get out of here."

With his arm around her shoulders, they stumbled into the woods and kept moving until the creek was well behind them and they could see the lights from Nicole's deck through the trees. Between them and the deck, a snow-covered bench, birdbath, and trellis marked Nicole's perennial flower garden. An unfamiliar black sedan was parked on the drive that wound around the house from the other side.

"Hold up," Jace said. Hannah stopped and they stood still, listening. "I don't think they're trying to cross the creek behind us."

"No," Hannah agreed. "It would make more

sense for them to go back to the truck and take the road around." She turned to him and touched his precious face. "That bullet—it could have killed you." The thought of losing Jace was even more terrifying than the rope bridge.

"But it didn't. I'm right here. We're safe." Jace smiled and pulled her into a tight hug. "We're both okay, thanks to you getting us across the creek."

She allowed herself one long moment in his strong arms before stepping back. "We're okay, but Nicole isn't. We've got to help her."

Jace straightened. "What's the plan?"

Hannah shrugged out of her pack and pulled out the globe that had caused all the trouble while she surveyed the area, then the holstered gun on Jace's hip. "We need to trade the coin for Nicole."

"I'll take it to him," Jace offered, but Hannah shook her head.

"He's expecting me, and you have the gun. You stay here and cover me. The security cameras should pick me up as soon as I get close enough to activate the motion light over the back deck." She pulled off her hat and laid it beside the pack. "I want to make sure he recognizes me."

"Good idea." Jace pulled the gun from his

holster, checked that it was loaded, and ordered Scout to get down and stay. "I'm ready."

"If anything goes wrong, call the police." Hannah took a deep breath and stepped out of the woods. She was still twenty feet from the deck when the floodlight came on. She stopped and held up her hands, making sure the globe would be visible to anyone looking at the security camera.

She waited, but no one appeared. She glanced in Jace's direction, but she couldn't see him in the shadows of the forest. Still, she knew he was there. She went forward, up the steps to the deck, knocked on the door, and then turned and hurried down the steps and away from the deck, where she would still be visible from the door but not so close someone could drag her inside. A few seconds later, more outside lights flashed on and the door opened a crack. Hannah got a glimpse of her sister's face, pale and terrified. Nicole stepped out onto the deck, but a tall man with blond hair was behind her, holding an arm around her throat. Hannah wasn't sure, but he looked like the man who had bought a gold pan last week. "I said not to call the cops," he shouted.

"I didn't," Hannah insisted.

"Then who's that in the woods?"

Hannah must have given it away when she

looked back for Jace. She straightened her shoulders and tried to control the quaver in her voice. "A friend. He won't stop you, as long as you do what you've promised." She searched her sister's face and body for signs of injury. "Are you okay, Nicole? Did he hurt you?"

"I'm okay," Nicole called back, but her voice sounded weak. "Just give him what he wants."

"I have it, right here." Hannah held up the globe. "Let my sister go, and it's yours."

He eased Nicole another step forward, and Hannah could see that he was carrying a gun in his other hand. "How do I know you didn't open the globe?"

"I did open it," Hannah admitted, "and I found the coin. It's still inside."

"Show me," he ordered.

Hannah nodded. "All right. I'm going to take out my phone now, because I need to look at the combination. Also, I'll need a pin. Okay?"

"Slowly."

With exaggerated care, Hannah opened her jacket and removed a safety pin. Then she took her phone from her pocket and found the photo Nicole had sent of the card that had been inside her jewelry box. Her hands shook, but she managed to press the right buttons and count the degrees of rotation, until finally the globe separated into two parts. She laid them on the snow-covered bench, and then held up the plastic box containing the coin. "Here it is."

"What's the date and mint?"

She squinted in the low light. "San Francisco, 1854."

"All right." The man shifted his grip on Nicole's neck. "Put the coin in the globe and walk away."

"Not until you let Nicole go."

"I'll let her go once I have the coin."

Hannah shook her head. "How do I know you won't take the coin and a hostage?"

"How do I know your friend won't shoot me the second I let her go?"

They stared at each other for a long moment. Then Hannah spoke. "Take me instead."

"Hannah, no!" Jace called out from the woods.

"It's okay," she called back. "Nobody has to get hurt." She took a step toward the kidnapper. "I'll walk with you to your car, and you can drive away with the coin."

"Stay there." The man shoved Nicole forward and down the steps from the deck, keeping her between himself and Jace. "Turn around," he told Hannah.

Slowly she turned her back on him. A second later, he shoved Nicole forward and wrapped his arm around Hannah's neck. "Show me the coin."

Hannah held up the coin, still in its box. The

man looked over her shoulder to read the in-
scription. "That's the one." He snatched it from
her hand and put it in his pocket. "Okay, we're
going to my car now, one step at a time." Something poked her ribs, and she realized it must be
the gun barrel. "Move."

THIRTEEN

Nicole ran toward the woods, momentarily blocking Jace's view of Hannah and the kidnapper. By the time Nicole was past Jace's line of fire, the kidnapper was already dragging Hannah toward the black car.

"Jace Angeles," Nicole whispered. "Is that you?"

"It's me." Without taking his eyes off Hannah and the kidnapper, he got out his phone and handed it to Nicole. "Take this. Hide somewhere in the woods and call 911. Tell them there's a kidnapper in a black sedan taking Hannah. I can only read the last two numbers on the plate: 74."

Nicole stared at Jace. "But he said he'll let Hannah go."

"He'll say whatever it takes to get what he wants. If he thinks he's safer with Hannah, he'll take her along. Also tell the police to be on the lookout for a white pickup in the vicinity. The two men inside shot at us earlier."

Nicole still didn't move, other than a violent trembling. She was dressed in jeans and a sweater, no coat, but Jace guessed it wasn't the cold that was giving her the shakes. Nevertheless, he didn't have the time to help her with her shock right now. He spoke in a gentle but firm voice. "Listen, Nicole, I know you've been through a lot, but you need to be strong for a little longer. I need you to find somewhere safe and make that call. For your sake and for Hannah's. Can you do that?"

Nicole stared at him for a second and then said, "Yes." She moved farther into the woods out of his sight. Jace continued to watch the kidnapper and Hannah. They were almost at the car now, with the man still hiding behind her, only his pale hair and the side of his face visible. They reached the car and as he opened the door, he said something to Hannah. He seemed to be relaxing his hold on her. Good, he was going to leave her behind.

But before the man made it into the car, the sudden roar of an engine and slamming doors announced a new arrival at the front of the house, and the kidnapper grabbed Hannah once again.

The two men who had broken into Hannah's rental car in Fairbanks burst around the corner of the house waving guns. The big guy still wore his green parka. The other guy spotted the two halves of the globe lying on the bench. He knocked them to the ground and shouted to the kidnapper, "Where's the coin?"

The kidnapper had his own gun up and pointed in their direction. He'd released his hold on Hannah, but now she was right in the line of fire. "You're too late, Rocky. Back off."

"I don't think so." Rocky stepped nearer.

The big man in the green parka caught up and took a few menacing steps toward the kidnapper. "Hand it over, old man."

"Let's talk about this later, shall we? I'll just hold on to it for now—"

"That's not going to happen," Rocky said. "If you haven't noticed, you're outgunned."

All three of the men looked as though they could start shooting at any moment. Jace watched helplessly, willing Hannah to move away, but the three men surrounded her. Her eyes darted from face to face, but none of the criminals seemed inclined to back down.

Sirens sounded in the distance. Rocky swore. "We gotta get out of here." He nudged his cohort forward. "You grab Ivan, and I'll take her. Throw them in the truck. One of them has the coin." He moved toward Hannah.

Jace's heart jumped into his throat. Scout whined. Jace reinforced the stay signal. The last thing he needed was for Scout to jump into the middle of this. Or was it? In sudden inspiration, Jace grabbed the hat Hannah had left beside her pack and showed it to Scout. "Find!"

Scout bounded forward from the woods. The men stopped and all eyes turned to the dog as he rushed into the middle of the crowd, cutting off Rocky's path to Hannah. As soon as the dog reached Hannah, he jumped up, knocking her to the snow and out of Jace's line of fire. Jace stepped forward into the light, pointing his pistol at the three men. "Everybody freeze!"

Surprisingly, they all did. Three pairs of eyes glared hard at him. "Drop your guns," Jace ordered. The blond kidnapper and the big guy from the white truck obeyed. Rocky dropped his gun, but then made a dash toward the front of the house. Jace let him go. He ordered the other two men to turn around and put their hands behind their heads.

In the front, the truck engine roared to life. The big guy from the white pickup spit out a curse. But before the white pickup could leave the house, police cars came dashing up the long drive with flashing lights and sirens.

Meanwhile, Hannah managed to get out from under Scout and crawl toward Jace. Scout followed, wagging his tail over this new game. Once Hannah was away from the two criminals and out of Jace's line of fire, she got to her feet.

"Are you okay?" Jace whispered, not daring to take his eyes off the two men long enough to examine her.

"I'm fine," she told him. "Thanks to you and Scout." She ruffled the big dog's ears and looked around. "What happened to Nicole?"

"I'm here." Nicole came out of the woods. "Oh, Hannah. I thank God you're okay."

Hannah opened her arms and the two sisters hugged.

"Police!" came a call from the side of the house.

"We're in the back!" Jace shouted. "Hurry!"

Police appeared from inside and around the edge of the house; guns drawn. "Sir, drop the pistol."

"Gladly." Jace dropped the gun and held up his hands.

It didn't take the police long to sort out who was who and handcuff the two criminals. Judging by the sirens, more emergency vehicles were on their way. Jace removed his coat and handed it to Hannah. "For your sister."

"Thanks." Hannah draped the down jacket over Nicole's shoulders. "Can we go inside?" she asked the nearest police officer.

"Let me check on that." He disappeared around the corner of the house.

While they waited, Hannah set the globe aside, brushed the snow from the garden bench

and urged Nicole to sit. Two emergency technicians came from the front of the house. They
returned Jace's coat, wrapped Nicole in a warm
blanket, and took her vitals.

"I'm fine," she insisted, but her voice sounded
as though she was trying to convince herself.

"Your blood pressure is high," the first EMT
said. "I think we should get you checked out at
the ER."

"That's not necessary," Nicole started to
stand, but then sat back down with a thump.
"Whoa, did everything just spin around for a
second?"

Hannah rested a hand on Nicole's shoulder.
"You'd better go in and get checked. You've been
through a lot." Hannah's eyes were bright with
tears. "I'm so sorry I didn't come that night when
you called."

"I'm just glad you're all right." Nicole sniffed
and turned to the EMTs. "Okay, let's go." With
the EMTs supporting her on both sides, Nicole
walked toward the ambulance. Jace and Hannah followed.

One of the technicians noticed his limp. "Are
you injured, sir?"

"I just wrenched my knee. I'm okay."

The man nodded. "RICE. Rest, ice, compres-
sion, and elevation."

"Good advice. Thanks." As they neared the

driveway, they could hear Rocky claiming in a loud voice that the police had no grounds to arrest him. "I was looking for my buddy's house, and I turned into the wrong driveway. Get these cuffs off me!"

An officer was listening to something on his radio. He nodded to the one who was standing with the handcuffed prisoner. "Outstanding warrant in Fairbanks. Hit-and-run."

"There you go." The second officer nudged the prisoner toward a waiting police car. "You have the right to remain silent…"

The EMTs took Nicole to the ambulance, loaded her up, and told Hannah where they were taking her. "I'll be there as soon as I can," Hannah promised. As she watched the ambulance make its way down the drive, Jace slipped an arm around her shoulders.

"Oh, Jace," she whispered. "I—" A sob interrupted whatever she had been about to say, and suddenly all the tears she must have been holding back over the past few days broke loose.

"Shh." Jace pulled her into his arms. "It's all over. You're safe now."

She wrapped her arms around his waist and held on as though he was the only thing keeping her from falling into an abyss, but through her tears he heard her whisper, "Because you kept me safe."

* * *

Late the next morning, Hannah balanced the tray she was carrying and tapped on the un-latched door of her guestroom, causing it to swing open. "Nicole?"

"Come in." Nicole pushed back the quilt and mumbled. "What time is it?"

"Time for elevenses." Hannah set the tray on a small table near the window and poured tea from the pot into two mugs.

Nicole yawned. "I can't believe I slept so late." She sat up and propped an extra pillow behind her.

"You needed it." Hannah gave her a mug. "You couldn't have gotten much sleep over the past few days."

"No," Nicole admitted as she accepted a blue-and-yellow flowered mug with a handle shaped like a carrot. She took a sip and then raised the mug and squinted at the bottom. "Is this Spode?"

"Good eye. It's Imperial Garden." Hannah gestured toward the matching teapot. "Isn't it cute, the way the pot looks like it's made of cabbage leaves?"

"And the handle on the lid is a butterfly. That's adorable." Nicole took another sip. "Where did you find it all?"

"Garage sale, believe it or not, marked three dollars for the full set. Something they'd found in an aunt's attic." Hannah offered a plate of tiny shortbread cookies. "I paid them thirty-five."

"You're too soft." Nicole laughed and took a cookie. "Where's Jace?" Once Jace and Hannah had finished with the police, they'd borrowed Nicole's car and gone to meet her at the emergency room. By the time they'd arrived, the doctor had already examined Nicole. With her blood pressure lower if not completely back to normal, he'd released her, and they'd all spent the night at Hannah's house.

"I drove him to the airport early this morning," Hannah answered. And she had been missing him ever since. Considering all she and Jace had been through together, saying goodbye was never going to be easy, but at least it had been relatively drama-free. On the drive to the airport, they'd chatted about the weather, Scout's upcoming training, and the locally made handicrafts Hannah carried in her store. In the chaos of finding a place at the curb to drop him off and the other drivers hovering behind, waiting for the space, there wasn't time for more than a quick hug goodbye. No promises of "see you soon" or "keep in touch." They'd never even exchanged cell phone numbers, Hannah realized with a pang. But she kept her voice casual as she added, "He had to get back to Fairbanks.

Some sort of supply chain emergency he had to sort out."

"Oh." Nicole gave Hannah an appraising glance. "How long have you and Jace been…?" Nicole waved the cookie around vaguely before popping it into her mouth.

Hannah shook her head. "We're not together. Jace just happened to be walking his dog at the ice park in Fairbanks when those two guys in the white truck broke into my rental car and tried to take my backpack. He ran them off."

"You were lucky. And then what happened?" Nicole asked.

"And then he drove me to my hotel, but he spotted the same guys lurking around the parking lot, so I stayed at his house instead. The next day those guys had the road blocked off to the airport, so Jace convinced me to take the train with him, and then to stay at his cabin…" Hannah drew in a breath. "Oh, Nicole. I'm so sorry I didn't ride the train to Anchorage and come to your house that day like I'd promised. If I'd had any idea somebody was holding you hostage—"

"I'm glad you didn't. I felt horrible, trying to lure you into a trap like that. I almost blurted out he'd kidnapped me, but he had a gun, and the way he looked at me…" Nicole shuddered. "It was like he didn't see me as human at all. Just a pawn in a game."

Hannah winced. "And I just left you there, in danger. You even tried to tell me to call the police, talking about Grandpa's flag, but I was too dense to get the hint."

"It was a long shot. Besides, I suspect that if you had come and brought the coin that first night, he would have decided it would be safer for him if neither of us lived to tell the tale."

"That's a sobering thought."

"Yeah, well, I had a lot of time to think about it after I went and blabbed about the Angeles cabin, and he sent those two goons after you to find the coin. I could hear him on the phone, yelling at them that he didn't care about the weather, they should have waited for you at the cabin, forced you to give them the globe, and 'dealt with the problem.' It didn't take a lot of imagination to guess what that meant. He ordered them to go back the next morning, but they reported that you'd already left the cabin by the time they arrived, and they couldn't find you or the globe. He called them a few choice names and said they could just forget about getting a cut, that he'd handle everything himself from then on."

"I guess when we're thanking God for keeping us safe, we can add in thanks for sending in that windstorm early so they decided not to wait it out at the cabin. Was it the same two guys who showed up in the truck last night?"

"Had to be. He called one of them Rocky on the phone." Nicole ate another cookie.

"Rocky posed as a neighbor and tried to way-lay me on the way to the expert's house in Fair-banks. He and the other guy did a hit-and-run on the expert's pregnant daughter so that he would be tied up when I arrived."

Nicole's eyes widened. "Is she all right?"

"I hope so. Last I heard she was going in for an emergency C-section."

"I hope they both made it okay." Nicole took another sip of tea and set the mug on the bedside table. "So where is the coin now?"

"The police took it for evidence."

"Oh, duh, of course they did. What coin is it and why were those guys so desperate to get their hands on it?"

Hannah shrugged. "I don't know. You're the coin specialist in the family. It was gold, Amer-ican, but I don't know much more than that."

"Did you take a picture?" Nicole asked ea-gerly.

"You know, I didn't. We didn't figure out how to open the globe until the night before last when we camped, and we were using lanterns. We were in such a hurry to start skiing the next morning, it didn't even occur to me to take a picture in daylight." Not to mention those kisses in the moonlight that had driven every other thought from her mind. Nicole didn't need to know about that.

"You were camping? In a blizzard?" Nicole looked horrified. But then she'd never been one for spending time outdoors in less-than-optimal weather.

"No, the wind had died down by the time we left the cabin," Hannah assured her. "We had to ski out because they'd sabotaged the snow machines, and so we camped one night on the way to Pika."

Nicole shook her head. "I'm sorry I told them about the cabin and forced you to ski all that way and risk hypothermia sleeping outside in the winter."

"It wasn't too bad. Jace had a good tent and warm sleeping bags. I'm the one who should be sorry. I'm sure I was a lot more comfortable in that tent than you were with a kidnapper in your house."

"Stop." Nicole held up her hand, palm toward Hannah. "It's established that we're both sorry, and we both forgive each other. Can we stop apologizing and move on already?"

Hannah smiled. If Jace were there, he would be telling her the same thing, but in a more tactful way. "Absolutely."

"Okay, then. What did the coin look like?"

"Um, it had an eagle on one side."

Nicole laughed. "So do half the quarters in your cash register. You'll have to do better than that."

"Okay, let me think." Hannah closed her eyes and pictured the coin. "The eagle was holding arrows. Lady Liberty was on the other side, with stars."

Nicole sat up straighter. "Did it say Liberty on a coronet across her head?"

"I think so. Yes, I'm sure it did."

"What was the date and mint?" Nicole demanded.

"San Francisco mint." Hannah was sure of that. "The date was old, eighteen fifty-something."

"Eighteen fifty-four?"

"That sounds right. Why?"

"Because if it is, you actually held in your hand an eighteen fifty-four San Francisco Mint Coronet Half Eagle gold coin, one of the rarest coins out there!"

"Coronet Half Eagle. Why does that sound familiar?" Hannah mused.

Nicole was almost bouncing on the bed. "Because there were thought to be only three in existence, but in 2018, some collector in New England discovered a fourth one and sold it for over two million dollars. It was in all the news."

"Oh, wow. I do remember that story. They thought it was a forgery, but it turned out to be real."

"Yes, exactly. Which means a two-million-dollar coin might be sitting on a shelf in police evidence between a stolen bicycle and a baggy of drugs." Nicole shook her head. "I wonder, is this a fifth coin, or is it one of the original three?" Nicole patted the bedside table beside her tea mug. "Shoot, I don't have my phone. Can I borrow yours?"

"Sure." Hannah took the phone from her pocket, touched the fingerprint reader, and passed it to Nicole, who typed something into the search bar.

"Hmm." A line formed on Nicole's forehead as she read. "It says in the article that three of the four San Francisco eighteen fifty-four Coronet Half Eagles are in museums, and the other is in the hands of an unnamed private collector. You don't suppose Candace Linacott was the private collector? I mean, she obviously had a lot of money, but was she that rich?"

"I don't know, but she didn't seem to have multiple houses or private jets, that sort of thing."

"Never mind." Nicole scrolled down. "The private collector still has his, so this one must be number five. Still incredibly rare."

"You know, Jace and I wondered if the coin

might be tied to a robbery at the Anchorage airport a couple of decades ago. Let's see, I was in eighth grade, so you would have been in fifth. Do you remember hearing about it?"

"Something about a courier getting drugged? Let me look it up." It took a minute for Nicole to locate the original news story. "Yes, it says the courier was on his way to deliver five assorted valuable coins to a museum in Boston. He was found drugged in an airport bathroom with no coins and no memory of what happened. Let's see if there's a follow-up story that lists exactly what coins were taken." Nicole swiped through a few things on the phone. "I don't see anything about the coins, but if one of them was as yet an unknown Half Eagle, the museum probably didn't want it publicized that they'd lost something so valuable. Oh, no—a week later, the body of an airport employee who was a person of interest in this case was found in Centennial Park." She looked up. "You think Candace Linacott was involved in this robbery and murder? Why?"

"It's just a hunch. For one thing, she hid an extremely rare coin in a wooden puzzle box, which was hidden inside an ordinary chest of drawers with the drawer screwed shut. And that chest wasn't even stored at her house. I mean, there's no law that says you have to keep your valuables in a safe or vault—"

"But that would make a whole lot more sense, unless you were afraid someone might come with a search warrant and go through your safe looking for stolen property. If this is one of the coins from the robbery, I wonder what happened to the other four mentioned in the article? They could hardly be as rare as the one in the globe, although, they must have been quite valuable, too."

Hannah shrugged. "Sold to private collectors maybe? I suppose we should mention this theory to the police when we give our statements this afternoon."

Nicole made a tsking noise. "I'd say so, and we should ask what measures they're taking to keep that coin safe. What time are we supposed to be there?"

"I told them one o'clock."

Nicole threw back the covers. "In that case, I suppose I should get up and shower. I'm going to need to borrow some clothes until I can get back into my own house."

"Of course. Help yourself to anything in my closet." Hannah started to gather up the tea things, but she stopped and turned. "Nicole, I know we said we were done apologizing, but I really am sorry, and not just because of the kidnapper. It feels like I haven't been a very good sister for the past few years. I should have supported you more through your divorce, but my nose was out of joint because you opened your antiques store after I did. And since then, it seems like we've been more competitors than sisters. But when that kidnapper came on the phone and said he was holding you hostage—" Hannah pressed her hand to her chest. "I was so scared. I know we don't usually say things like this out loud, but I love you, Nicole. I don't know what I would do if anything happened to you."

"The truth is, well, I love you, too." Nicole's voice was shaky, and her eyes glittered with unshed tears. But then she grinned. "And talk about competitiveness, don't be hogging all the blame. I got so sick of hearing Mom go on and on about how well your shop was doing, I decided to show you up. That really is the only reason I opened my store—to spite you."

"But you're so good at it," Hannah protested.

"Running the store, or spiting you?"

Hannah snorted. "Well, both, actually."

"You're right." Nicole laughed. "Ironic, isn't it? It turns out that I really like running the store and looking for beautiful things like that Karas jewelry box. And there's an example of my competitiveness coming back to bite me. I was so eager to sell it for a profit to show you I didn't pay too much, I didn't bother to research the box and see who made it until after it was sold. I could have kicked myself when I went on-line and saw that it was worth eight thousand or more. Not that I was going to admit that to you. But I am sorry I outbid you on that box. And on the carnival glass, which I didn't plan to buy until you started bidding. I shouldn't have behaved that way toward you."

Hannah shook her head. "Why do we do this?"

"Habit, I guess." Nicole thought for a moment. "I think it goes back to Lindsay."

"Lindsay?" Nicole had never seemed particularly interested in Lindsay. If anything, she'd snubbed Hannah's best friend. "What does she have to do with anything?"

"I was always jealous because the two of you were so close. I felt like I was invisible. I guess I thought that if I could do things as well or better than you and Lindsay that you would accept me and let me into the club. But you never did."

Hannah thought about it. When she and Lindsay were seven, it made sense that four-year-old Nicole couldn't play board games or climb trees, but as they all got older, there was no reason they couldn't have included Nicole. But they never did. "You're right. We did exclude you. I'm sorry."

Nicole shrugged. "I got over it. But I have to

admit, it felt like payback watching you crushing over Lindsay's big brother, where you were the invisible one, instead of me."

"What are you talking about?" Hannah tried to keep her voice casual, but she felt her face getting warm.

"Are you really going to pretend you weren't head-over-heels in love with Jace all through high school? Like you didn't have his initials in little hearts all over the inside of your notebook? Everybody knew—everybody but Jace, that is. He was totally oblivious. My friends and I used to laugh about it." She gave a wry smile. "You can add that to the list of things I'm sorry for. Maybe we should be writing this stuff down."

"No need. I'll forgive you for snickering behind my back if you'll forgive me for ditching you."

"It's a deal. And by the way, I don't think I ever told you at the time, but I'm sorry about what happened to Lindsay. And I know you blamed yourself, but what happened to her wasn't your fault."

"Thanks." Hannah sighed. "Jace said the same thing at the cabin."

"Did he now?" Nicole swung her legs to the floor and shoved her feet into the slippers Hannah had loaned her, but she remained seated on the bed. "Just out of curiosity, is the spark still there?"

"What spark?" Hannah asked in her most innocent voice. She gave up the pretense. "How was he looking at me?"

"Like I would look at a Victorian ruby ring marked five dollars at a garage sale. No, scratch that. I'd buy that ring and sell it again, but Jace was looking at you as though you were the most precious thing in his world, and he would do anything to keep you safe."

"Well, that's just Jace. He would have helped anyone in trouble." If Nicole were right about Jace's feelings, he would have said something before he left town. Wouldn't he?

"You think so?" Nicole's expression was thoughtful. "I agree he would have come to the defense of anyone being mugged in a parking lot, but would he have whisked just anyone away to his cabin to keep them safe? Or risked his life confronting a gang of criminals to rescue just anyone's sister? The man is a store manager, not an action hero. It's not as though he was trained in any of this stuff. But when you needed him, he was there. Even though you hadn't seen each other for, what, thirteen years now? He cares about you."

Before Hannah could formulate an answer, Nicole stood and shuffled off toward the bathroom. But before she shut the door, she called over her shoulder, "I hope this time around, you plan to do more about it than doodle his initials inside your notebook."

FOURTEEN

Jace watched Scout scoop up a yellow tennis ball and execute a skidding about-face in the snow to bring it back for another turn. The dog would do this all day, given the opportunity, but Jace was on his lunch hour. It had taken him most of yesterday to straighten out the ordering mix-up with one of their suppliers. It might not have taken so long if he could keep his thoughts on business, but instead, his mind kept returning to Hannah.

When the store manager, Bette, had called early yesterday morning to tell him about the mess, he'd taken the excuse to return to Fairbanks. Bette had been working for Angeles Adventure Store for twenty years. She could have taken care of the problem, and she would have if Jace had been out of cell phone range at the cabin like he'd planned, but he'd flown home to handle it himself. Truth was, he was running away.

Seeing Hannah in danger, surrounded by

angry men with guns, he would have traded everything he owned and everything he was if it kept her safe, including his own life. And afterward, when he held her in his arms, the intensity of his feelings—well, they scared him. He wasn't an impulsive person. He might have known Hannah since she was six years old, but this adult version of Hannah was a virtual stranger. And yet, in a matter of days, she'd become the center of his thoughts, the center of his life. It was all happening too fast. It couldn't be real. He needed to put some distance between them.

Hannah didn't protest when he'd told her he needed to catch a plane to Fairbanks yesterday morning. She'd simply driven him to the airport and given him a goodbye hug. Which was good, right? Now that the criminals were locked up and the coin was safe, it made sense that he and Hannah should go back to their own separate lives. Only he was starting to think that there was no going back for him.

Scout nudged Jace's hand with the ball. "Okay. Just a few more." He threw the ball again and checked the time on his phone. Twenty minutes left in his lunch break. Not that anyone would question the boss if he happened to take a long lunch, but Jace liked to set a good example. Then he noticed today's date—his parents' anniversary. Shoot, he'd meant to mail a card Friday, but in all the excitement, he'd forgotten. He took out his phone and dialed. "Hi, Mom. Happy anniversary."

"Thank you! Just a second, and I'll get your dad and put him on Speaker." There were the usual beeping, bumping, and static noises that happened whenever his mom tried to make adjustments to her phone. "Russell. It's Jace."

Dad's voice came through. "Hi, son."

"Hi. Happy anniversary."

"Thanks." Jace could hear the smile in his dad's voice. "Hard to believe it's been thirty-nine years. Seems like yesterday when I spotted your mother across that crowded room—"

"It wasn't that crowded," Mom cut in. "And it wasn't a room. It was a backyard cookout and there were only eight people there."

"Were there eight?" Dad asked. "I only had eyes for one."

"Oh, you," Mom replied and Jace heard the smack of a kiss.

He grinned. His parents seemed to be treating their retirement as sort of a second honeymoon, and Jace wholeheartedly approved. "So, what are your plans to celebrate?"

"Nothing too fancy," Dad said. "We're going out to dinner with friends."

"And I got your dad tickets to a Boise State basketball game this Saturday," Mom added.

"Fun," Jace said. Mom had never been a particular sports fan until he made the team in middle school, and his parents had developed a sudden fascination with basketball. Lindsay and Hannah would come to every game, too, cheering so loudly Jace's teammates used to tease him. There he went again. It seemed as though every subject in his mind eventually led to Hannah.

Without giving any thought to the consequences, Jace asked, "Tell me, Dad. How long from the time you met Mom until you knew she was the one you wanted to spend your life with?"

"Honestly?" Dad said. "Ten minutes. Twenty, tops."

"Oh, phooey," Mom exclaimed. "He didn't even ask me out for three weeks after that cookout."

Dad chuckled. "Jace asked when I knew, not how long it took me to work up the courage to do something about it. Why do you ask, son?"

"Yes, why? Did you meet someone special?" Just from the tone of Mom's voice, Jace could almost picture her raising her head like a bird dog finding a scent. For years, she'd been hinting that it was time he settled down and started a family.

"Not exactly," Jace hedged. Hannah was definitely special, but he hadn't just met her.

Of course Mom wasn't going to let that go. "You did! I can hear it in your voice."

Dad snorted. "Are you sure that voice you're hearing isn't your own inner wannabe grandmother?"

"Like you're not just as eager to be a grandfather," Mom countered. "Tell us about her, Jace."

Jace hesitated, but then he decided to go for it. Maybe his parents could give him some insight. And besides, he needed to fill them in on what had happened before they heard it elsewhere.

"I was walking Scout at Ice Alaska on Friday, when I heard this woman yelling in the parking lot. Some guy was chasing after her and knocked her down. Scout and I ran over, and the guy jumped into a white truck with his partner and took off. They'd broken into the woman's car and stolen her suitcase."

Dad said, "Thank goodness you were there."

"Yes." Jace took a breath. "The woman was Hannah Yates."

"Hannah?" Mom gasped. "Our Hannah?"

"What other Hannah Yates would he be talking about?" Dad asked. "What was Hannah doing at the Ice Sculpture place? As far as I knew, she hadn't been back to Fairbanks since high school."

"It's kind of a long story," Jace said, "so get comfortable." He told them all about the events of the last few days. Except, of course, for those moonlight kisses. That was between him and Hannah.

"Hannah crossed a rope bridge?" Dad marveled. "When she was in high school, she wouldn't even hike to the waterfall with us because of the ledge along the trail, and that ledge is a good six feet wide."

"I know. She's still scared of heights, but with a whole lot of praying, she did it. Just like when she climbed down into the ravine after me."

"That was very brave of her," Mom said thoughtfully. "Is your knee better now?"

Jace smiled to himself. He could always count on his mother to worry about his health. "My knee is fine. I just wrenched it a little when I fell."

Mom sighed. "I hate that you put yourself in danger, but I'm glad you were there for Hannah. Poor girl. That must have been terrifying to have those men chasing her. And then to find out her sister was being held hostage—it doesn't bear thinking about."

"It was scary," Jace admitted. "But Hannah was amazing. You should have seen the way she handled herself with the kidnappers."

"But I'm confused," Mom said. "Why does Hannah run a store? She was going to study nursing at Arizona State."

"She never went to Arizona. You know the plan was that once she and Lindsay graduated, they were going to explore the country together as traveling nurses, but Hannah said it just didn't feel right without Lindsay. Hannah ended up getting a business degree from UAA, instead. She opened her antique store in downtown Anchorage a few years ago. It's called Hannah's Alaskan Treasures."

"But I thought..." Mom stopped talking, but Jace knew exactly what she'd thought—that Hannah had gone on with her plans without a backward glance for her friend. Mom sighed. "You know, I was just thinking about Hannah the other day. I was not kind to her that night at the hospital, sending her home like that."

"You were upset," Dad said soothingly. "I'm sure Hannah understands."

Jace wasn't so sure. "Hannah and I talked about Lindsay, there at the cabin. Hannah has been blaming herself all these years. That's why she never got in contact with you after the funeral. She thought you didn't ever want to see her again."

"Oh, dear. I wish I'd called to apologize, but by the time I was together enough to do that, Hannah and her family had moved away to Anchorage, and I never bothered to try to find them.

I should have. Hannah may have covered for Lindsay, but the accident was not her fault."

"I know, and I told her that. When we were at the cabin, we took one of those rocks Lindsay had painted—you remember the one with the eagle—and we carried it to the creek where Lindsay and Hannah used to like to go to watch the otters. We had a little memorial service for Lindsay there."

"That's so sweet. So Hannah never forgot Lindsay."

"Never," Jace assured her.

"Would you text me Hannah's phone number?" Mom asked. "I'd like to call and clear the air, let her know I never really blamed her. I was just lashing out."

"Sorry, I don't have it," Jace said, "but I'm sure you can reach her at her store."

"What do you mean you don't have her phone number?" Mom demanded. "Why not?"

Jace had been wondering the same thing. "I don't know. It just never came up."

Mom continued to press. "How are you going to move forward in this relationship if you don't have her phone number?"

Were they going to move forward? Jace was in Fairbanks; Hannah was in Anchorage. They had just spent an intense weekend together, but were these feelings real and lasting? "I'm just not sure—"

"Yes, you are," Mom interrupted. "You just haven't worked up the courage to do something about it yet. Like father, like son." Mom laughed. "Hannah may have made a mistake, but she was one of the sweetest girls I ever knew, and pretty, too. I'm sure she's grown into a lovely woman, inside and out."

"She has." Jace couldn't deny that.

"Then you'd better stop dilly-dallying and make your move," Mom said. "Women like her don't come along every day."

"Jace is old enough to make his own decision about whether he wants to pursue a relationship," Dad pointed out.

"Well yes, but—"

"Judy." Dad's voice held a warning note.

"Fine. I know you'll make the right choice, Jace. I'll be praying for you. And thanks for the call. It makes our anniversary even more special to know you've found your someone."

"Judy—" Dad repeated.

Mom laughed. "Love you, Jace."

"Love you, too. Bye, Mom. Bye, Dad." Jace hung up the phone.

He called Scout and returned to work, where he sat at his desk and got nothing done. He was supposed to be reviewing the latest and greatest new adventure gear to decide what to order for next season's inventory. Ordinarily this was one of his favorite tasks, but he just couldn't seem to concentrate today.

He'd been at it for an hour when Bette walked into his office. "I wanted to apologize for yesterday. When I called about that order problem, I was thinking you were at the Anchorage store and could handle it from there. I forgot you'd taken the week off. And I sure didn't mean for you to have to fly home and ruin your vacation. I should have taken care of it myself."

"That's all right. It was my decision to come back early." He'd chosen to run to Fairbanks, to put some distance between himself and what he was feeling. But the feelings hadn't gone away. No, the more he turned it over in his mind, the clearer it became. He'd fallen in love with Hannah Yates. It was as simple as that. Question was, did she feel the same?

"Are you planning to fly down for the grand opening Saturday, or are you going to drive tomorrow?" Bette asked.

"Oh, wow. That's the day after tomorrow, isn't it?" It seemed like a year ago when Jace had scheduled a driver to meet him in Pika early Saturday morning and take him to Anchorage for the event. "I'm going to drive." He closed his laptop. "In fact, I'm going home now to pack, so

I can drive down this evening. I have some important personal business in Anchorage tomorrow before the grand opening on Saturday. You can handle things here, right?"

"Of course," Bette told him. "Just out of curiosity, does this important personal business in Anchorage have anything to do with a certain antiques store owner there?"

He looked up. "You've been talking to my mother, haven't you?"

"Now why would you think that?" Bette winked. "I always did like that girl. Such a sweetheart. Can't wait to see what kind of a woman she grew up to be. Godspeed, Jace."

Jace grinned. "Thanks, Bette."

FIFTEEN

Friday morning, Hannah stacked a new selection of pillowcases on a table in one corner of the store, while Sue Ann unlocked the front door and turned the sign to Open. A minute later Tracy Schmidt, a regular customer and a friend of Sue Ann's, wandered in and immediately gravitated toward a carved cedar chest Hannah had just set out. Yesterday, Hannah had responded to an online listing for that chest, only to find when she arrived to purchase it that the chest was stuffed with hand-embroidered pillowcases, tea towels, and aprons that the seller had forgotten were there. Knowing how much her customers loved handmade items, she'd negotiated a price for the whole collection.

Sue Ann went to help Tracy, so Hannah just called a greeting. Once she'd finished laying out the pillowcases, she slipped through the curtain into the workroom where she set up an ironing board, started the iron preheating, and switched on her radio. Once the iron was hot, she reached into a basket for one of the aprons she'd washed last night, this one pinafore-style with daisies embroidered across the top.

She spritzed some water onto the apron and ran her iron over the cotton fabric, enjoying the homey smell of freshly ironed cloth. Music played in the background, a modern instrumental interpretation of a favorite old hymn. It was good to be home, good to be back into her normal routine, and yet, Hannah felt unsettled. Sue Ann would say that was to be expected after such a frightening experience, but Hannah didn't feel particularly skittish or nervous, just…off. As if she'd forgotten an appointment or left something behind.

Like maybe her heart.

Hannah sighed. Nicole might or might not be right about Jace's feelings, but she was correct about one thing: Hannah was no longer a teenager, doodling Jace's initials in her notebook. What she felt toward Jace wasn't some girlish crush. In the brief time they had spent together, that spark of attraction had caught and grown into a full-fledged bonfire.

But what was she going to do about it? Jace was in Fairbanks. She was here. Eventually, when the police were done, they would return the globe to her and she could see if Peter Morozov was still interested in having her bring it to Fairbanks, but that could be months, and she didn't want to wait months to see Jace again.

Of course, there was always the chance that Jace didn't share her feelings. Yes, he'd kissed her out there in the wilderness, but that might have had more to do with their situation than with any deep feelings. A few kisses didn't necessarily mean he wanted an ongoing relationship. And even if he did, there was the matter of Lindsay. Jace said his parents had forgiven Hannah, but forgiveness was one thing. Having the person you held responsible for your daughter's death dating your son was a whole other matter. The last thing Hannah wanted was to come between Jace and his family.

She closed her eyes in a silent prayer. Was it God's will that she and Jace should be together? Could they work out things with his family? When she opened her eyes, she still wasn't sure. But she knew she had to try.

Maybe she should give him a call, just to check on him, feel him out a little. She didn't have his cell phone number, but she could surely reach him through the store. But that didn't feel right. When she talked with him, she wanted to see his face, and not in a tiny picture on her cell phone. She wanted to touch his hand. If all went well, she wanted to put her arms around him and feel his kiss.

The song on the radio ended, and a commercial came on. Hannah ignored it, until the words "grand opening" caught her attention. The announcer was talking about special promotions and door prizes for people attending the Angeles Adventure Store grand opening tomorrow. Jace would be there. In fact, he might even be there now, helping prepare for the big event.

Maybe she could drop by this afternoon, ask for him, and casually offer to take him out for a meal after closing. It would be a friendly, supportive thing to do. And if he agreed, it would give her a few hours to gather up her courage before she laid her heart on the line. The very heart that was beating faster at the thought of seeing Jace again.

She hung up the freshly ironed apron and pulled another from the basket, but paused before she picked up the iron. Why wait? She could drive over right now. If Jace wasn't there, she could try again tomorrow. She paused just long enough to unplug the iron, run a brush through her hair, and apply a fresh coat of lipstick before grabbing her coat, but before she could let Sue Ann know she was going, the bells on the door rang, signaling a new customer. Hannah glanced at the employee schedule on the wall.

Cheryl wouldn't be in for another hour. Hannah shouldn't leave Sue Ann alone in the store, not after all the scary things that had been happening.

With a sigh, Hannah set her coat aside and stepped through the curtain into the store. A man wearing a down jacket had his back to her while he examined one of Charlie's wooden rolling pins. The man's dark hair, waving a little where it met his collar, almost looked like...

A dog stepped out from behind the display and woofed a greeting in her direction—a big fluffy yellow dog. Jace turned and flashed that gorgeous smile of his. "Hannah!"

"Jace!" She hurried toward him. "What are you doing here?"

He caught her in his arms and Hannah's heart swelled. She wrapped her arms around him and breathed in his warm, woodsy scent.

"I got into town late last night, but somehow I never got your phone number," Jace told her as he released her from the hug. His hands ran down her arms and lingered, his thumbs moving over the backs of her hands in little circles. "So, I thought I'd drop by and see if you might have some free time to spend with me today."

"I, uh..." Hannah couldn't seem to form a coherent sentence when he was touching her hands like that.

"She's free now." Sue Ann sidled up to them, a knowing smile on her face. "Hi, I'm Sue Ann Bolton, Hannah's store manager, and I'm guessing you're Jace Angeles." She offered her hand.

"Yes." Jace dropped Hannah's hands so that he could shake Sue Ann's, and Hannah immediately felt the loss.

"I thought so. There aren't too many people who can leave Hannah speechless and blushing." She chuckled. "And this must be the famous Scout, who ran into the middle of a crowd of gun-toting kidnappers and knocked Hannah down and out of danger. I know I'm not supposed to interact with service dogs when they're in their vests, but I really want to give that dog a big hug."

"It's all right," Jace told her, "as long as the handler gives permission. Scout, go say hi."

The dog went to Sue Ann, who heaped him with extravagant compliments and petting. Tracy joined her, and soon Scout's mouth was open in a doggy grin and his fluffy tail kept bumping against a nearby table leg hard enough to rattle the dishes on top.

Hannah stood next to Jace and watched, grinning. After a few minutes, Jace laughed. "Okay, enough, or you'll be spoiled rotten. Come, Scout." The dog returned, and Jace snapped on the leash.

Sue Ann smiled. "Next time, I'll have a treat for him. Now, Jace, why don't you and Hannah go get some coffee or something? I can handle the store."

"Cheryl doesn't come in until eleven. Are you sure you don't mind working alone?" Hannah asked.

Sue Ann waved away her concerns. "I've got this. Y'all have fun."

"It will take me a while to look through all the new goodies, anyhow," Tracy said, "so Sue Ann won't be alone."

"All right. Thanks. I'll get my coat." Hannah ducked into the back and grabbed her jacket and bag. When she returned, Jace reached for the jacket and held it while she slipped her arms inside. Once she'd buttoned it, they stepped out the front door and he reached for her hand. Neither of them had bothered with gloves, and his hand warmed hers. Scout walked along on his other side. "Where did you want to go?" Hannah asked.

"I'm not sure." He glanced down at the dog. "As a service dog in training, Scout is allowed in restaurants, but I don't usually take him because there's not always a lot of room for a big dog like him."

"Why don't we just grab coffee and walk around Town Square?"

"Sounds good to me." As they strolled along the sidewalk, Jace mentioned, "I talked to Peter Morozov yesterday. You'll be glad to know his daughter has recovered from the hit-and-run, and that she and his grandson are at home and doing well."

"That is good news." They reached the coffee shop a block from Hannah's store. Their walk-up window was closed in the winter, so Hannah popped inside to get them two cups of coffee. She came out and handed one to Jace. "Sugar, no cream, right?"

"Thanks." He looped Scout's leash over his left wrist and transferred the cup to his left hand, leaving his right free to reach for hers, lacing their fingers together and tucking their joined hands inside his coat pocket to keep warm. This was nice, Hannah decided. She could get used to it.

"Have you found out any more about whether the gold coin is tied to that airport robbery like we thought?" Jace asked before he took a sip of coffee.

"It is indeed. The police have it for now as evidence, but once they're done, it will go to the museum where it was originally headed. The coin is—let me get this right…" Hannah closed her eyes briefly to concentrate. "…an 1854-S Coronet Half Eagle, worth more than two million dollars."

"That's amazing. And to think you were carrying it around in a backpack."

"I know. And you remember when we were talking about that walrus ivory scandal? Turns out Ivan Penca, the guy who kidnapped Nicole, spent six months in prison for that crime. He must have gotten a nice reward for accepting the blame and keeping Candace Linacott out of it. As for the two guys in the white truck, Rocky Pearson and Alfred 'Tiny' Lima, they're falling all over themselves to talk to the police, trying to get the best plea deal by implicating the others. It seems they were all involved in the airport robbery. Ivan bribed an airline employee to find out which flight the courier would be on coming into Anchorage. At the airport bar, Ivan distracted the courier while Rocky put some drug in his drink. Once the courier began to feel the effects, Tiny escorted him to a bathroom off the main level, robbed him, and left him there. Later, to make sure the airline employee didn't talk, at least one of the three—depending on who is telling the truth—murdered him and dumped his body in Centennial Park. And it was all under the direction of Candace Linacott."

"Wow."

"I know. Since it all happened at the airport, the Feds have taken over. They suspect once they dig a little deeper, especially into Ivan's travel history, they may be able to clear up several smuggling cases as well."

"What happened to the rest of the coins that the courier was transporting?" Jace asked as they crossed Fourth Street.

"Nobody seems to know, but it's assumed Candace Linacott sold them to private collectors and that's where she got the money to pay Ivan, Rocky, and Tiny. Together the other coins were worth about a hundred and fifty thousand according to the police report. It seems odd that she held on to this one for so long instead of selling it, but maybe she was waiting for just the right collector who would pay top dollar."

Jace thought about it. "Or maybe she got a thrill from possessing something so rare."

"If so, it might have cost her. Her death was listed as cardiac arrest, but I understand the investigators are considering exhuming the body. But if it turns out Ivan and company had anything to do with her death, between the original crimes and the new robbery, breaking and entering, and kidnapping charges, it's going to mean very long prison sentences for the three men involved," Hannah said.

"Just as long as it keeps them far away from you." Jace squeezed her hand. "What about the globe puzzle box?"

"Good news. It seems that, since it was in the

chest of drawers I bought, it's legally mine once the police are done with it." They reached the corner and Hannah pushed the crossing button at the light.

"Are you going to sell it to Peter Morozov?"

"I haven't decided yet." She was tempted to keep it. True, the globe was a reminder of the danger they'd been through, but it had brought her back to Fairbanks and thrown Jace into her path, and she could only be grateful for that.

The light changed and they crossed the street and followed one of the pathways that meandered through Town Square. The snow glistened in the sunlight. A couple skated together on the small rink in the center of the square. Mounds of snow covered the beds that city workers would fill with a riot of bright bedding plants in the summer, making this one of Hannah's favorite places in Anchorage.

"That sun feels good," Jace commented, pausing to let Scout sniff at a lamppost.

"A little warmer than Fairbanks?"

"Much warmer. It's supposed to be nice for our Anchorage store's grand opening tomorrow."

Hannah nodded. "I heard your commercial on the radio. Sounds like the grand opening is going to be a lot of fun."

"I hope so. I'm looking forward to it, but that's only partly why I'm here. Once the grand opening is behind us, I want to explore the possibility of moving our headquarters to Anchorage."

Hannah's breath caught. She stopped to face him. "Would that mean you're thinking of moving here?"

"That's the plan."

She grinned. "Are you getting so soft you can't take the weather in Fairbanks anymore?"

He chuckled. "Better weather is just a bonus." He dropped Scout's leash, told him to stay, and took Hannah's cup and set it on the snow next to his. Then he took both of her hands in his and looked into her eyes. "The reason I want to move to Anchorage is because I want to be close to you. I believe that you and I could have a real future together. That is, if you're interested."

She couldn't imagine anything she wanted more. But had he really thought this through? "What about Lindsay? And your parents? Will they be able to forget what I did? Won't Lindsay's accident always be there, between us?"

"Lindsay would be thrilled with the idea of us together. You know she would. She'd probably be picking out her maid of honor dress even as we speak."

Hannah laughed. "She already did, in eighth grade. Purple, with a chiffon skirt and sequined bodice. You know how she loved sparkles."

"She really did." He stroked Hannah's cheek

with his finger. "I've talked with my parents, and they're completely on board with the idea of you and me together. My mom feels horrible about those things she said to you at the hospital. She wants your number so that she can call and tell you herself. So, how do you feel about what I said? Are you interested in having me around?"

She closed her eyes for a moment to savor the feel of his caress before opening them again. "I'm interested. But tell me more about your plans for us."

"You mean long-term or today?"

"Either. Both." She laughed, just for the joy of it. "Let's start with today."

"Okay. Depending on your schedule, I was hoping that we could spend some time together. Maybe catch a movie, then hit the diner and have breakfast for dinner. Or we could do some ski-ing or skating or..." He leaned closer. "Maybe some kissing."

"Kissing, you say?"

"You know. Like this." He brushed a soft kiss across her lips. Then he slipped his arm around her waist and pulled her closer.

She reached up to take his face in her hands and look into his eyes. "It's all so amazing." She smoothed a lock of hair from his forehead.

"What is?" Jace asked.

"That you and I should find each other again,

after all these years." She raised her face for another kiss, but Scout's keen ears must have picked up the word *find*. He jumped onto the two of them, knocking them onto the relatively soft snow on the flower bed next to the path. Jace rolled as they fell so that Hannah landed on top of him.

Scout tried to crawl onto the pile, but Jace pushed him away. "Are you okay?" he asked Hannah.

"I'm fine." She laughed as she got up. "You're still protecting me, I see." She offered a hand.

"I'll always protect you." He took her hand and allowed her to pull him to his feet. "I love you, Hannah. I didn't think it was possible to fall in love this fast, but I was wrong. I really do love you."

"Oh, Jace." Her hand flew to her chest. "I love you, too!"

"That's the best news ever." He gave Scout a stern order to sit and stay. "Now, where were we?" He opened his arms.

Hannah stepped into them and threw her arms around his neck. "I believe we were right about here."

And this time when they kissed, no one interrupted for a good long time.

SIXTEEN

Five months later

Hannah flashed her exhibitor pass and wheeled in a dolly with two boxes stacked on top of a mid-century nightstand past the gates of the Alaska State Fair in Palmer. She paused for a moment to breathe in that distinctive fair scent: fried food, farm animals, engine grease, cotton candy, wet grass, and a hundred other aromas she couldn't name. Whenever she caught a whiff of that smell, she was instantly ten years old with a clutch of ride tickets in her pocket and Lindsay at her side, eager to see, taste and experience everything.

She smiled, remembering. She did that now, whenever she thought of Lindsay. Instead of the sadness and guilt she used to feel, she remembered the fun, the laughter, the sheer joy that Lindsay brought to life, and she was thankful to have had such a friend.

She moved slowly along with the crowds, admiring the flower gardens, 4-H exhibits, and Irish dancers performing on an outdoor stage. Soon she reached the vendor area and rolled her dolly past tents selling fireweed jelly and birch syrup, chainsaw sculptures, and specialty soaps, until she came to the bustling Angeles Adventure Store tent. She stopped and parked the dolly out of the way. Several store employees were interacting with customers. Jace was at the back of the large tent, talking with a young couple about the two sea kayaks he had on display.

She'd only been watching him for a few seconds when Jace looked her way, almost as though he could sense her presence. He shot her a smile and held up a finger to indicate he'd be just a minute. Hannah nodded and crossed the tent to a portable dog run where Rosy, Jace's currently assigned service dog in training, was holding court.

Rosy, a six-month-old labradoodle puppy, had already mastered all her basic obedience commands and leash manners. If Rosy had possessed a pinky finger, it would certainly have been raised while she sipped tea with the queen. Since she was a puppy, however, she contented herself with greeting her adoring public with wiggles and tail wags.

Hannah reached into the pen and tousled the

red curls on the puppy's head. With her sharp brain and unflappable disposition, Rosy would be a blessing in the life of some special person someday, just as Scout would help save lost hikers and avalanche victims. It had been hard on both Hannah and Jace to send Scout off to "dog college" as Jace called it, but Scout's new trainer kept them up to date. According to her, Scout was progressing well, and she had finally managed to convince him that he didn't need to knock people down in order to rescue them.

Jace walked over to Hannah. "Hi, there." He leaned in for a kiss.

"Hi. I didn't mean to interrupt your sales pitch. I was just on my way to take a shift at our booth and thought I'd stop by and let you know."

"I'm glad you did. I'll be done here and ready for dinner at about six. Can you take a break then?"

"I should be able to if Nicole can cover for me." Hannah and Nicole had decided to combine their resources and share a booth at the state fair this year, something neither of them had tried before. So far it was working out well, with a higher sales volume than either of them had anticipated.

"All right then," Jace said. "I'll meet you at your tent, and we can grab a couple of corn dogs and some chili fries."

Hannah wrinkled her nose. "You mean halibut tacos and funnel cakes."

"Do I?" He grinned. "We'll negotiate later. Mom and Dad are planning to drive out this evening, by the way. They'll probably stop in at your booth." After one more quick kiss, he went back to the couple and the kayaks.

Hannah pushed the dolly past a dozen more tents that sold everything from hot tubs to jeweled dog collars before arriving at the tent with Nicole's "Hillside Heirlooms" banner hanging above her "Hannah's Alaskan Treasures" one. Nicole had won the coin toss on whose banner went on top, but it really didn't matter because they'd mixed their inventories together. Nicole's beaded shawls were draped over a ladder beside Hannah's antique dressing mirror, and Hannah's curio cabinet displayed a set of Nicole's hand-blown glass goblets.

When Hannah checked, it looked like both the goblet set and the curio cabinet had sold, along with quite a few other items. Good thing she'd brought in some replacements. Sue Ann was busy counting out change to a woman with a whole stack of baby quilts. Nicole was a few feet away, lifting a tray of vintage brooches from a locking jewelry case to allow a man a closer look. Several people browsed, looking over Nicole's porcelain figurines and Hannah's quirky salt-and-pepper shakers.

After waving a greeting to Sue Ann and Nicole, Hannah made her way toward the back of the tent, unloaded the nightstand, and opened the boxes. Even before she'd finished unpacking, a woman with dark curls had snatched up one of the antique garden gnomes. A slightly older-looking woman, who wore a "Made in Alaska" ball cap, complained, "Hey, I wanted that one."

"Too bad. I got here first." The curly-haired woman smirked.

"Brat," the first woman retorted.

Hannah got the impression the two knew each other well. In fact, based on the similar shape of their eyes and noses, they were most likely sisters. Nicole caught Hannah's eye and smiled. Hannah knew just what she was thinking. That could have been the two of them, not long ago. Their relationship had come a long way in the last few months. Hannah unwrapped another gnome. "I've got more."

"Ooh, let me see." The ball cap woman picked it up. "I like the colors in this one better anyway."

"The hat matches the trim on my house. Let's trade," her sister suggested.

"Not a chance." With a smug smile, the older sister paid Sue Ann for the gnome. The curly-haired sister waited for Hannah to finish unpacking the other three she had brought, but after dithering between them for a good ten minutes, she decided if she couldn't have the one her sister had bought, she didn't want one at all.

Once she was out of earshot, Nicole whispered to Hannah, "She'll be back for that first gnome if she can figure out how to ditch her sister. If she buys it in front of her, her sister will gloat about getting the best one."

Hannah laughed. "Sisters."

"I know, right?" Nicole accepted the box of glass paperweights that Hannah had picked up at her store and turned to arrange them on top of a mahogany ladies desk. "Is Jace here?"

"He's working the Angeles Adventure tent. Okay if I slip off for a little while around six? He said he'd be ready for dinner then."

"No problem. Sue Ann says she's bringing her sister to help later, so we can cover."

For the next two hours, Hannah was too busy helping customers and couldn't talk with Nicole or Sue Ann, but around five thirty, traffic slowed as people switched their attention from shopping to food.

Sue Ann took her dinner break. "I'll be back by six, and my sister, Leigh, will be here then, too, so you can take a break," she told Hannah before she left.

Nicole sold her current customer a garnet ring, but once she'd gone, they had no shoppers for a few minutes. Hannah noticed faint dark circles under Nicole's eyes. "You've put in a long day," Hannah told her. "Why don't you head out? I can cover the booth."

"I'll wait until Sue Ann is back from dinner break at least," Nicole answered.

"That's not necessary. It's slow, and Sue Ann is bringing her sister-in-law to help."

But Nicole wouldn't budge, so Hannah stopped asking. Maybe Nicole wanted to be here, around people. Hannah knew Nicole had met with the prosecutors managing the kidnapping case against Ivan Penca earlier that morning, but she hadn't had time with Nicole since then to ask how it went, and she didn't really want to do it now, when they were sure to be interrupted. It had to be hard for Nicole, anticipating coming face-to-face with her kidnapper in court and having to field questions from his defense attorney. Maybe she hadn't been sleeping well.

Hannah had an appointment with the prosecutors the next week, so she should get a better idea of what to expect then. In the meantime, she should schedule some downtime with Nicole, just the two of them, to talk about it. Or not. If Nicole didn't want to talk, they could just get coffee or something, whatever would help

Nicole feel better. At least Rocky and Tiny had already accepted plea deals, so Nicole and Hannah wouldn't need to testify at those trials.

Hannah was refolding and stacking quilts when someone tapped her on the shoulder. She turned to find Judy and Russell Angeles smiling at her. "Hi, there!" Hannah leaned in for a hug, careful not to jostle Judy's giant tote bag. She hugged Russell, too, who was carrying three more shopping bags. "Looks like you two have found lots of goodies. Want me to stash your stuff so you don't have to carry it around?"

"That would be great." Judy passed over the heavy tote with a relieved sigh.

"Now that I have a hand to carry it," Russell said, as he gripped the shopping bags, "I'm going to get some lemonade. Anyone else want some?"

"Not right now, thanks," Hannah answered, and the others declined as well. He went off toward the food vendors while Judy admired a needlepoint stool.

Hannah tucked their bags into a locking trunk she had hidden under a table with a tablecloth that reached the ground. Jace's parents had spent most of the summer in Alaska, much of it at Jace's new home in Anchorage. Hannah had been a little apprehensive the first time she faced them again, but Judy had given a sincere apology for what she'd said at the hospital, and they had been nothing but welcoming and friendly to Hannah ever since.

Nicole was showing a woman her collection of Victorian hatpins when her phone rang. After glancing at the screen, she told the customer, "Excuse me, I need to take his call. Hannah, can you take over?"

"Sure." Hannah stepped behind the jewelry counter and smiled at the woman while Nicole walked away from the tent. "Any particular ones you'd like to see?"

"How about that one?" She pointed to one with an egg-shaped jade top.

Hannah removed the heavy eight-inch pin from the velvet pincushion and handed it to the woman.

The woman eyed it warily. "Kind of dangerous looking, isn't it?"

Judy drifted over to see the pins. "I read that Victorian women sometimes used their hatpins as defensive weapons."

"Interesting," Hannah said. "No wonder they were popular if they could look this pretty and function as a weapon." It was too bad Nicole wasn't carrying a hatpin when Ivan had kidnapped her. Hannah noticed a shorter silver one and plucked it out of the pincushion. "Look at this lily of the valley design."

"That is pretty. May I see?" The customer handed back the jade pin and took the silver one, discreetly checking the price tag. "I'll take this one. My aunt collects old hats, so I think she'd like the hatpin to go with them."

"Who wouldn't? It's lovely," Judy commented, while Hannah wrapped the pin in tissue paper and put it into a gold organza bag along with Nicole's business card.

Hannah ran the woman's credit card and handed over the bag. "Hope your aunt loves it."

Nicole returned, but instead of asking about the sale, she gazed into the distance. Hannah studied her sister's face. "Everything okay?"

Nicole looked at Hannah and blinked. Then she smiled. "Everything is great, actually. Ivan Penca accepted a plea deal, after all. I won't have to testify."

Judy gave Nicole a hug. "That must be such a relief."

"It is, for sure," Nicole replied.

Hannah took a turn hugging her. "I'm so glad."

A voice behind them asked, "So, are those hugs for just anyone or only for your sister?" Jace had arrived, with Rosy on a leash beside him and a paper sack from the fish taco stand in his hand.

"You brought me halibut tacos. You get double hugs." Hannah wrapped her arms around him and gave him a kiss before releasing him. "I thought you wanted corn dogs and chili fries."

"I did, but once I smelled the halibut frying, I decided you were right. But then, you usually are."

Hannah laughed. "I'm going to remind you that you said that. We were just celebrating because Ivan Penca has accepted a plea bargain and Nicole won't have to testify at the trial."

"That is good news." Jace sent a sympathetic glance Nicole's way. "So it's all over."

"It's all over," Nicole repeated. She flashed Jace a little smile. "On to the future."

"Absolutely." He gave a quick nod.

Hannah wasn't quite sure what that was all about, but she didn't have time to think about it because Jace took her hand. "Let's find a picnic table before these tacos get cold."

"Can you wait just a minute? Sue Ann isn't back yet."

"I'm here," Sue Ann called as she walked up from the other direction. "And I brought reinforcements." Sue Ann's friend, Tracy, and her sister, Leigh, both regulars in the store, trailed after her. "Y'all go ahead and have dinner. We've got this."

"Thanks," Hannah said after greeting the trio. "Nicole, Judy, are you coming with us?"

Nicole shook her head. "I want to jot down a couple of notes for inventory and then I'm heading home. I'll see you tomorrow."

"You go on ahead," Judy told Hannah and Jace. "I'll catch up with you after Russell gets back."

"Okay. Have a good night, Nicole. I'll see the rest of you later. I'll be back in half an hour," Hannah promised.

Jace waved goodbye and tugged Hannah along to the seating area where he found a picnic table and set down their food bag. "You hold the table and I'll get us some drinks." He studied the menu printed on a nearby booth. "Pineapple express soda or black bear lemonade?"

"That's a mixed berry lemonade, right? I'll have that."

Jace handed Rosy's leash to her and went for the drinks. Rosy, who wouldn't dream of begging at the table, settled herself under Hannah's bench. Jace returned with their drinks and Hannah handed him a taco from the bag before unwrapping her own. Creamy lime chipotle sauce dribbled from the edge, and she licked that up before biting into tender beer-batter halibut chunks and crunchy cabbage shreds. Delicious as always.

They talked about the successes of their booths and what they might want to change next year while they ate. Once Hannah had finished the last bite of her taco, Jace asked, "Ready for that funnel cake?"

She shook her head and put her hand on her stomach. "I couldn't eat another bite. Maybe later." She stood and stuffed napkins into the bag. "I should get back to the tent."

Jace checked the time on his phone. "You've got a while before they're expecting you. Let's walk a little."

"All right." Hannah couldn't turn down any chance to spend time with Jace. They wandered through the midway, watching happy kids on the carnival rides while Rosy in her vest trotted along beside them. Soon, they were walking past the carnival games.

Jace stopped in front of a booth with rows of balloons attached to the back wall. Stuffed animals and other prizes dangled from the rafters. No one else was at that booth just then. "Think I can pop a balloon with a dart and win you a prize?" Jace asked Hannah.

"I've no doubt you could, but you don't need to. I have everything I need right here." Hannah squeezed his hand. "Besides, they probably don't use real darts anymore. Too dangerous for kids."

The proprietor, who must have been getting something off a lower shelf, straightened up and spoke. "We use beanbags now," he told them. "There's a tack in back of the balloon that will pop it if the beanbag hits in the middle of the balloon. But hey, you can use a dart if you want to. Five bucks a throw." He reached under the counter and pulled out a single dart. It looked to be the same brand as the darts at the Angeles cabin.

"Sounds good to me." Jace handed over a fiver.

There was something off here. Why would the proprietor have just one dart available? Didn't this game usually give multiple chances? "What do you win if you pop a balloon?" she asked.

The man shrugged. "You have to pop the balloon to see. It depends on what the paper inside says."

"Here goes," Jace said before Hannah could ask any more questions. The dart sailed through the air, straight at a red balloon in the corner. Pop. A square of paper floated to the floor.

The proprietor bent down to pick it up and read it. Hannah expected him to reach for one of the toy harmonicas or stuffed animals hanging from the rafters, but instead he leaned over to pull something out from under the counter. He handed a small blue box to Jace.

Jace, in turn, opened the box and pulled out

a ring. "Do you suppose it's a real diamond?" he asked Hannah.

Hannah grinned, and looked at the trinket he was holding. Then she took a second look. Three clear stones in the center of the ring sparkled like fire, set on an old-fashioned filigree band the color of rose gold. It was rose gold!

Suddenly, Jace dropped to one knee. "Hannah, ever since I saw you that day at the ice park, my life hasn't been the same. It's been a thousand times better. I love you, Hannah, and I want you in my life forever. I promise to stop at all garage sales and to move heavy furniture for you whenever you ask. Will you marry me?"

He signaled to Rosy, and she sat up on her back legs, her front paws dangling and the expression on her face absolutely adorable.

Hannah gasped and pressed her hand to her heart. "Oh, Jace. Every day I thank God for bringing you into my life. You kept me safe when I was in danger, and you've brought me more happiness than I could have imagined. Yes! I would be honored to marry you."

Jace stood and she let him slip the ring onto her finger before she threw her arms around his neck. Someone cheered, and she looked over to see Nicole, Sue Ann, and Judy clapping and jumping up and down while Russell recorded everything on his phone.

Strangers joined them, stopping to cheer and clap for the proposal. Hannah grinned and waved. Then she held up her hand to inspect the ring. "It's beautiful!"

"Your sister helped me find it. We both thought it was just your style, classic, graceful, and strong." He kissed her forehead. "Just like you."

"I love it! And I love you."

Nicole, Sue Ann, and Russell all came to hug and congratulate them. Judy waited until the others had moved on to Jace before she approached Hannah and took her hand to admire the ring. "Oh, sweetie, I'm so happy to have you in our family." She chuckled. "I'm going to tell you a secret. When Lindsay was, oh, eight or nine, she came to me and said, 'Mama, I want Jace to marry Hannah when we grow up, and then she'll be my sister forever and always.' And I laughed, but in my heart, I prayed that Lindsay's wish would come true. And now God has answered my prayers."

"Judy, that's so sweet." Hannah tried to blink back tears as she pulled Judy into a hug.

"What's this?" Jace came over. "Mom, are you making my fiancée cry?"

"Happy tears," Hannah assured him as Judy stepped back. He put an arm around Hannah's shoulders, and she wrapped hers around his waist. "Jace, I can hardly wait to be your wife. To be part of your family and to make you part of mine. Together, forever and always."

"Forever and always," he agreed. And he kissed her once again.

*****

Dear Reader,

I hope you've enjoyed spending time with Hannah and Jace in Alaska. I've been fortunate enough to call Alaska home for more than thirty years now, and I'm thrilled to be able to share my Alaska with you. Every morning when I look out my window at the Chugach Mountains, I'm in awe of God's creation.

But God's creation didn't stop with the mountains, the oceans, and the stars. God created us, and He told us to love one another. Sometimes, our relationships become strained, like Hannah's relationship with her sister, Nicole, or with her best friend's family. But God blesses us, and by His grace we can learn to forgive and love, just as God loves us.

I love to hear from readers. You can find my contact information or sign up for my newsletter at www.BethCarpenterBooks.blogspot.com.

Blessings!
Beth Carpenter